# MEXICAN MOON
# AND OTHER STORIES

## Karen E. Taylor

OTHER BOOKS BY

KAREN E. TAYLOR


THE VAMPIRE LEGACY SERIES:

Blood Red Dawn

Thirst

Crave

Hunger


CELLAR


THE PRESENCE

## PROVENANCE

"VampWare" first saw print in *100 Vicious Little Vampires*, published by Barnes and Noble Books in 1995.

"The Blood of the Rose" first saw print in *100 Wicked Little Witches*, published by Barnes and Noble Books in 1995.

"Romeo Falling" first saw print in *Return of the Dinosaurs*, published by Daw Books in May 1997.

"Forever" first saw print in *Horrors!: 365 Scary Stories*, published by Barnes and Noble Books in 1998.

"Mexican Moon" first saw print in *Daughter of Dangerous Dames*, published by Twilight Tales in May 2000.

"Freedom" first saw print in *Brainbox: The Real Horror*, published by Dreams Unlimited in October 2000.

"A Good Idea at the Time" first saw print in *Women Writing Science Fiction as Men*, published by Daw Books in June 2003.

"Angel," "The Calling," "Contacts," "Dancing the King Stag's Moon," "The Debt," "One Green Candle," "Two's Company, Five's a Crowd" first saw print in *Fangs and Angel Wings* published by Betancourt and Company in November 2003.

"The Tips of Her Wings" first saw print in *Small Bites*, published by Coscom Entertainment in August 2004.

All other material is new and copyright 2015 Karen E. Taylor

Cover Design © 2015 Melanie Fletcher

# TABLE OF CONTENTS

*I blame the fabulous Bernini sculpture of The Ecstasy of St. Theresa*

*for this one.*

## ANGEL

A word unspoken

Held only in my soul,

Whispered in fevered nights to unhearing ears.

Until my lips were opened

And it flung itself to the floor,

A breathless homage to one who felt he deserved it not.

Theresa had her angel,

The sweet piercing of breast,

An ecstasy and pain, unseen by all others.

Did she deny his arrow

Or open wide her heart,

And her unworthy arms and legs to welcome his thrust?

You are my angel,

A blessing and a cross.

Created with invisible wings, soft, silky and dark,

To fill the void in my soul,

To cover my nakedness,

To wrap around and bind me and give me to the wind.

*This story was started and finished several days after the death of my brother, Larry. One of the funeral home attendants was named Adams and he very kindly took me on a tour of their facilities. I'd planned to discuss some of the more gruesome embalming details he told me as well as include a scene with the two main characters in one of the below-stairs rooms. Sometimes what we plan isn't always the best thing for a story.*

## BLOOD OF THE ROSE

The first time Adam saw Marie she was seated by the side of her husband's casket. She made an oddly composed widow, dressed all in black, complete with hat and gossamer veil that did not quite hide her somber smile and the predatory gleam in her eyes. Her hands rested, smooth and reassuring, along her gently expanded abdomen and she held court with visiting relatives and friends like a queen.

He knew all about her, of course, her age, her address, even her credit rating. But the neatly completed information form she had given the funeral director days before had not prepared him for the utter shock of her menacing beauty, the black eyes and perfect olive complexion that seemed to shine through her veil. The sharpness of her gaze was like the cold whisper of a scalpel against his skin and slashed him where he stood in his obsequious pose in the far doorway.

"Maintain the distance," his boss, Louis Bowe, owner of the Bowe Funeral Home, always said. "Think of yourself as a highly paid and valued servant, because that is what you are. Comfort should be offered, but with dignity and grace. We are the detached, sympathetic voice of reason in an insane world."

But Marie's eyes beckoned him into her insanity and he fell, moving across the distance of the outer room, propelled through the inner room, almost as if dragged through the crowd of mourners and the overwhelming display of funeral roses to a suddenly vacated space at her side. "Mrs. Zenos?" His ordinarily composed, detached voice cracked slightly to his embarrassment. "I'm Adam Rose. Allow me to express my sincerest condolences on your bereavement."

She held her hand out and he touched it briefly. Her skin was smooth, hot. "Mr. Rose," her voice was a rich deep contralto with a faint touch of a Greek accent, "thank you. I understand that you did the work on my Stephen."

So much meaning was encompassed by her words, "my Stephen," a love and devotion almost beyond his comprehension. But the eyes that considered him through the veil were dry and eager. He cleared his throat. "Yes, I hope you are satisfied with our results, Mrs. Zenos."

"Indeed, I am, most pleased," she reached over and tenderly stroked the cold arm of her husband, "we have all been saying that he looks so well, so alive." Her hand lingered caressingly on the corpse and Adam blushed, thinking suddenly and unavoidably of that hot skin pressed against his own. "You have done well."

He nodded briefly. "I'll be here for the remaining days of viewing, and of course for the funeral service. And if there's any other way I can be of assistance, please ask for me."

Marie smiled at him, exposing perfect, tiny white teeth. "You may be sure I will do that, Adam."

The next two days of viewing Stephen Zenos' body seemed to Adam to fly by in a feverish rush. Surrounded by a throng of mourners, swathed in black and shrouded in the heavy scent of the flowers, Marie watched him as he tended to his duties. Her black eyes continually followed him, as he played escort to elderly women and men, steering them to vacant chairs and whispering dignified words of comfort; her eyes studied him as he pressed endless glasses of cool water into reaching hands and sought him out as he delivered and rearranged the continual onslaught of bouquets.

The flowers were all roses; he'd thought that a coincidence on the first day, but with each new arrangement an odd and ominous symmetry was being established. The other attendants laughed about "The Rose Funeral" in hushed, but irreverent tones, speculating on Marie's apparent interest in Adam. "Maybe we should put you into a vase, too, Adam, and deliver you to her."

And he would blush and they would laugh even harder. But he didn't laugh, couldn't laugh. Everywhere Adam went, she was there, her rich voice rising over the other voices, her hands either caressing the dead skin of the corpse, or clasped possessively over her stomach, where Stephen's child rested. Over those two days, he grew to hate the corpse and then even the child, jealous for the touch of those hands.

The last night of viewing he lingered in the office, waiting for the mourners and family to depart. Mr. Bowe was present that night and Adam had made himself as unobtrusive as possible, fearing his fascination with the widow might be noticed. When Bowe finally entered the office, he smiled at Adam. "Good job, son. I'm going home, now. Close up for me, will you?"

Adam nodded, "Yes, sir." The front door opened, then shut and the faint sound of Bowe's car faded as it pulled out of the parking lot. Silence descended on the rooms; Adam shuffled some papers, then put them aside and stood up, stretching and yawning slightly.

Turning out the light, he closed the office door and started down the hall to the viewing rooms, to put them in order before the morning.

He gasped when he entered the room where Stephen Zenos' body lay. Marie stared up at him from where she sat, cross-legged in the middle of the floor, her dress billowing around her, surrounded by a circle of flickering votive candles. She had removed her hat and veil and was reaching into the basket positioned next to her, pulling out several dark round objects and lining them up carefully in front of her. "Adam," her smile sent an anticipatory thrill through him, "I know this is most likely a little unorthodox, but it is an old family tradition. Humor me. In fact," she smiled deeper, her eyes boring into his, her small hands beckoning, "do more than that. Join me, Adam."

"But," he hesitated at the edge of the candles' circle, "I shouldn't, or you shouldn't . . . be here, I mean."

Marie laughed, "Ah, but it is only you and I and Stephen here, now, and he won't tell a soul. Join me, Adam."

He stepped into the circle and sat down, overwhelmed by the aroma of the roses, the candles and her. "It is a beautiful scent, isn't it, Adam? Stephen loved my candles. I mold them myself, mixing the wax and the essences according to very old customs. My mother taught me when I was just a girl." She picked up one of the objects in front of her, held it up to her face and inhaled, then handed it to him. It was a plum, the outer skin so dark it seemed black in the candlelight. "Stephen's favorite fruit," her eyes, no longer hidden by the veil, were beautiful and reflected the flicker of the flames. "Eat," she urged him, selecting a plum for herself and biting into it. The juice ran over her chin and she wiped it away with the back of her hand, laughing.

Adam sat on the floor and stared at her, lightheaded from the scented air. The plum rested in his palm, forgotten and uneaten, until she gave another laugh and guided his hand to his mouth, pressing the cool skin of the fruit to his lips. "Eat, Adam."

His teeth burst through the surface of the plum; the skin was tart and crisp, but the center so sweet it brought tears to his eyes. He rolled the fruit in his mouth, savoring its texture, its flavor. He saw as he pulled his hand away that the plum's flesh was colored a deep red, as red as the roses, as red as blood, as red as Marie's lips as she urged him to eat more. Adam finished, sucking the last shreds from the pit, embarrassed by the sticky juice that now coated his fingers and his lips.

Marie laughed again, and pulled his hand to her mouth, licking the fingertips, then leaned into Adam and kissed him. His head reeled with that kiss, with the heady scent of the candles, the roses and Marie, with the cloying taste of the plum and her tongue. And when the kiss was done, she held his head between her palms. "Ah, my dear, do you know how long I had to search for you? How many funeral homes I had to call to find a Rose like you?"

He shook his head, he felt drunk, drugged with her presence. She smiled, stood up within the circle of the candles and slowly began to unbutton her black widow's dress. Adam could only stare as she slid it from her shoulders, as she shed her bra, her hose, her black satin panties. When she stood naked in front of him she reached her hands down to pull him up to her. He rose on unsteady legs, his eyes still fastened to her, admiring the swollen breasts, the soft curve of her stomach where the child rested. She was beautiful, the most beautiful woman he had ever seen and she wanted him, she said, she'd been searching for him.

He opened his mouth to speak, to say that he loved her, but could only produce a strange garbled sound. "No, don't try to talk," she reached down into her basket again, pulling out something long and shiny, "it won't help. Old family traditions, Adam, are so important. So very important. The candles, the roses, the plums, all prepared especially for you. My mother was a powerful woman, and bequeathed that power to me. Power over life and death," Marie laughed as she brought the knife to his throat, "yes, even power enough to bring back the dead. All is ready now, but for the final step. To bathe my Stephen's body in the blood of a rose."

Louis Bowe was surprised early the next morning to discover Marie Zenos waiting for him by the locked doors. "Mr. Bowe," she smiled sadly and touched his hand, "I have decided that I do not wish a final viewing this morning. All my goodbyes were said last night and I do not want the coffin open again. Let him rest now, safe from prying eyes."

"Whatever you'd like, Mrs. Zenos, we are here to serve your needs."

"And that you have, Mr. Bowe. I have been satisfied." Marie's voice dropped lower, "most satisfied."

Bowe shook his head slightly when a man emerged from the Zenos car and came to stand next to Marie, gently cupping her elbow in his hand. Such an uncanny resemblance to her late husband, he thought briefly as he unlocked the doors and escorted them inside. But he didn't give it much consideration, thinking only how glad he'd be to see the end of this funeral; the smell of the roses was stronger this morning, made his eyes water and his head ache. He hoped that Adam would arrive soon. It was not like him to be late.

*This one was commissioned by the West Suburban Symphony in Hinsdale, Illinois, to be read at their Halloween Opening Gala during a performance of "Danse Macabre" by Camille Saint-Saens. In order to write this very short but extremely difficult piece, I listened to a CD of the music over and over again, often phrase by phrase, so that I could get the words, intonation and timing just right. Printed here is the first version of the story and the one I like best; the second and performed version was much gentler in nature and the narrator was switched from female to male, to accommodate the actor who did the reading.*

## THE CALLING

I am old, almost beyond all reckoning. Tired, beyond all age. When the tower clock strikes twelve, it will be time for the calling. My steps are quiet and sure.

Power! It flows through me, pulls me along the path, beckons me deep within this dark place.

This place is real and yet not real, more false and yet truer than life. Here, bonds that have been severed in the world still hold tight.

Three will do. Three will complete the calling. I have called before, to each separately, and each has answered and done my bidding. Not willingly, not gladly, but I called and you were forced to answer, to work my will, my evil. Weeping in the night.

Listen. For now, I call again. Do not fail to answer.

My mother, the first. I draw you to me, caressing the bond that holds us together. Come forth.

"Look on me and weep," you say, "for I held the power. As did my mother before me. And I gave the power to you."

As a child I did not weep. Instead, I watched and learned.

Your voice said the words and in halting breaths I followed. Your hands sketched the runes and mine danced along. Into the power.

Further and deeper I delved. I grew and learned and triumphed.

Sure now, I grasped the power and took it deep within me, embracing the sky and the earth. Wanting more, I entered where you forbade me to go, learning secrets you would not teach.

Alas, my mother, the cost was your life. Before my eyes, you withered, growing as brittle and dry as old bones.

I consigned those bones to the earth, scattered the dirt from your final bed, and wept.

Not for long; youth is callous and there was more for me to learn than words and symbols.

A detour from the path then. Not wise, but necessary. I cast spells of soft flesh and tossing head, of words whispered in the sweet perfume of a summer's night. And too late, I was caught in the snare I myself had spread.

"Look on me and weep," you say, "for I was your only love."

Now, my lost love, the second. I stand and call you to me. Appear before me, and follow, follow me, further down the path.

Come forth and rise out of the darkness.

Love was not wanted, not wise, but I desired you more than power, more than life. You gave me a love song, a slow dance, granted me a surrender. A giving of a new magic. And for a while I gave and the magic grew.

But power feeds pride and I grew cold and drove you away, into the magic that belongs to men, the spell and allure of sharp steel and spears. The trumpets of war called for you then; my pride would not ask you to stay. You followed after another mistress, the field of battle. And then you were gone. Torn from me. I scattered the dirt over your broken body and wept, moving back down the path.

From love, though, came another. A daughter, from your death a life born.

"Look on me and weep," you say, "for I was your flesh and blood."

I call you to me, little one, broken one, the third calling, tugging at the bonds that hold us together. Rise and stand before me.

You lived for light and I led you into darkness. You wept and pleaded and I did not hear. I pulled you into the night and watched as the power flowed into you, held the knife that opened you. You denied the power, you refused the darkness and all that flowed was your blood.

Stand before me now, all three. And follow.

To the center of this place, this dead place, this dark place. And you whisper around me, you ghosts of my dead, my loves.

Grow stronger now, flesh forming from dust, hands reaching, hands grasping long, sharp knives of moonlight.

Mother, I bare my head before you.

Lover, I bare my neck before you.

Daughter, I bare my heart before you.

I call for justice for the dead. From the dead. Justice and penance for the evils I have done.

Come now, spirits of my calling and do not deny my will. Tear my soul from my body and fling it to the depths of darkness.

Look on me, I say. I have called you here to me.

Look on me, I say, for I loved you and wronged you. You must be avenged.

Three knives raise, three knives lower. I fall to the ground, cradled once again in arms that love me more than death and darkness.

Look on me, I say, and weep no more, for I am dead.

And the calling is ended.

*I guess we've all been to a few conventions, haven't we? I've a huge stack of cards collected in bars at cons over the years. And one never knows when those contacts will prove useful.*

## CONTACTS

It had been a normal convention. You've been to one, you've been to a million. Doesn't matter what product is being sold; sales is sales. Widgets or washers or waistcoats, it's all the same to a good salesperson.

"Which is what I am." When I glanced up at the rear view mirror, a pair of very tired looking eyes peered back. Not surprising, I thought, I had spent most of my time in the bar. Making contacts. What was demonstrated in the display area was secondary to the discussions in the bar. This trip, as usual, I returned with a full pack of business cards, my personal notation scrawled on the back, classifying each person and their potential worth.

I smiled to myself as I mentally thumbed through the stack, pausing every now and then, contemplating a remembered face. There were some good ones in this group, quite a few likely prospects. The boss would be pleased. "Contacts," he'd say with that devilish grin on his face, "are the most important thing. Don't ever forget it."

I was still smiling as the flashing red and blue lights pulled up behind me, then beside me. The policeman motioned me over to the side of the road and I obeyed with a sigh, reaching next to me to pull my license from my purse. As I did so, I hitched my skirt a few more inches up my thighs.

I rolled down my window. "Something wrong, officer?"

He leaned into the car, staring openly and unashamedly at my nylon-clad legs. "Well, that all depends, Miss. We have reports of a car of this type being stolen. I'd like to see your license and registration."

He examined the documents under the beam of his flashlight. Turned them over in his hands and examined them again, all the while sneaking looks at me.

I took advantage of his interest and leaned into him, inhaling deeply and repeating, "Something wrong, officer?"

"Well," he gave me another side glance, "I don't quite know. I wonder if you'd mind accompanying me to the station, so that I can check these out on the computer."

I sighed again and got out of the car. "Anything I can do to help, I will. But you might want to be advised that I have contacts, good contacts."

He grunted, and settled me into the back seat, locking the doors and climbing back behind the wheel of the cruiser. "Oh, I'm quite sure you and your contacts will be a big help."

He drove silently to the exit, through the provincial town, past the police station and populated areas to a small clearing. I could see shadows of maybe six other men, half-concealed in the trees. I shook my head as I realized what the set up was, remembering all too late the safety lessons for a woman driving alone. He pulled me from the car and cuffed my hands behind my back. I struggled just a bit as he dragged me over to the forming circle of men, not because I thought it would do any good, but on basic principles. "Caught us a fighter, did you, Jim?" one of the men called out and I gave a small laugh. Looked up at the policeman and batted my eyelashes.

"Don't I at least get one call, officer?"

He snorted. "Call away, Missy. I doubt it'll do you much good."

"Ah," I said, pulling myself up to my full height, "I wouldn't be too sure about that. You might want to cover your ears, though, this won't be pleasant."

He gave me a puzzled look as I threw back my head and called out a name, unrecognizable to them and unpronounceable with the human tongue. A tall shadow curled up out of the ground in the center of the circle and the men began to wail at the sight, trying to gasp out half-remembered prayers of childhood.

I shifted out of the cuffs and back into my normal shape, rubbing a pleased hand over the mottled, warty red skin I ordinarily wore. Smiled at my boss as he devoured this unexpected bonus.

The last to disappear into the mouth of hell was the policeman. He went feet first, screaming, his face distorted in fear, totally unappreciative of my parting remark.

"Contacts, officer," I showed him the grin I had learned from my master, "are the most important thing. Don't ever forget it."

*This story was written for a shared-world anthology that never came out, but even without the companion stories, I feel it's one of my best. I'll admit that I'm a bit of a sucker for the personification of Death, to say nothing of ancient folk festivals held under the full moon of October.*

## DANCING THE KING STAG'S MOON

The great square in Morobrany was never deserted.

Even the pre-dawn hours that Mikal preferred for his practice were moderately populated: vendors positioning their wares to catch the first morning traffic; skulking, shadowy forms pursuing illicit interests; and countless others, completely insubstantial, following patterns formed in life and exercised in death. Those with a tangible form avoided contact with Mikal, familiar as they were with his preoccupation and his habits. The ghosts, as was their wont, ever unfaltering in their paths, merely passed right through him.

Mikal took even less notice of them at this moment than usual, absorbed as he was in his physical movement, his attempt to attune his human body to the immortal music of death and life and the procession of the seasons. An attempt that seemed to be doomed to failure. He stumbled slightly and cursed as he glanced at the setting moon. Two weeks until the Festival of King Stag and he had come up with nothing. Should have kept quiet at the council meeting, Mikal thought, as he retrieved his tunic from where he'd tossed it before practice, and let the men do what they always did for this festival. "But no," he spoke out loud now, venting his frustration, shaking the dust from his tunic and throwing it over his shoulder, "Proud Mikal, the Master of the Dance wanted something special.

Something different. Something more meaningful than their typical drunken staggering."

He glared angrily at the few people in the square foolish enough to look back at him. "Better to muck out the stables in the Palace of Morobrany than to try to bring meaning into this dirty and Death-cursed town." Mikal realized too late that his words were ill-chosen, not ones to be spoken aloud. The people, visibly distressed, muttered amongst themselves. More care should be taken in talking of the patron god of Morobrany, a fact of life they could all agree upon; hadn't men's throats had been slit for less? And afterwards did it not happen that Death refused to collect their souls dooming them to restlessness for eternity?

Mikal had no fears of that happening to him. Not because he was a larger man than most of the townsmen, although he was. And not because he was meaner or tougher in a fight, he was in fact a peaceful man and preferred his solitude above all else. But Mikal had made his pact with Death many years ago and the depth of the resulting sadness and guilt protected him like a suit of heavy armor. Even though none knew his story, they perceived his otherness and kept their distance.

He gave a small, graceful bow and forced his lips into a half smile. His grief and frustration, after all, were not theirs to understand or share. "Forgive me, gentle folk, I should not have spoken thus. I bid you all good day."

Mikal turned and left the square, walking only a short distance before arriving at his stone house. At the door, he set his tunic down again and untied the leather strip that held his long black hair in place during practice. He dipped into the rain barrel for the cup and took a long slow drink, then reached in for more to pour over his head. The water was cold and invigorating and he shivered as it cascaded down his shoulders and over his naked, muscled torso. Still, he enjoyed the feeling and gave a low laugh as he shook his hair back.

A giggle answered him. "When you do that you are just like a horse in the rain."

The girl stood in front of him, too tall and too thin for her years, the color of her childhood faded. "Good morning to you, daughter, I didn't see you when I first arrived."

"I was hiding."

He nodded. "You are good at that." Then he shook his hair out again.

Another giggle escaped her lips, as he'd intended. "Oh, Papa, do you remember how you used to play the horse for me, before? What fun we had! I miss those days."

Mikal sighed and made a move as if to caress the top of her head, then slowly drew his hand back. There was no use in attempting contact. But he did smile. "Yes, my little Letni, I do remember. And yes, they were wonderful days." He glanced around the narrow street. "Now let us get inside out of this cold air."

He opened the door and entered his house, not looking to see if she followed. She came and went as she desired and he had quit trying to understand her reasons. Children had no logic, most especially a child like Letni.

Larger than most in the area, the house was clean and bleak, almost barren. Mikal's needs were few; he had a cot upon which to sleep, a table and two chairs, a hearth for heating and cooking, a small chest in which to keep his clothing. A few well-worn, handwoven reed rugs adorned the cold stone floor by his bed. The mats were the handiwork of Mikal's dead wife and should have been thrown away many years ago, but when he looked at them, he was reminded of a time when life made sense and death was not yet a god. He cherished those memories, picking at them like a scabbed wound. How long? Mikal thought, how long will it continue to hurt?

"Letni," he called, crossing through the empty half of the house devoted to his calling, to the table in his living quarters. Breaking off a large piece of dark bread, he called again, "I'm having breakfast, daughter, will you join me?"

There was no answer. He shrugged and gnawed on his bread, not really hungry, but knowing that his body needed some nourishment. It had been a particularly difficult practice this morning.

"Papa?" She was back again. He often wondered where she went when she disappeared. "There's a man coming to the door.

"Do we know him?"

"He's that musician. He was here yesterday when you were out and I forgot to tell you. He didn't see me..."

"Yes, I know, little Letni-cas. You were hiding."

"Shall I let him in, Papa?"

But Mikal was already at the door; he opened it and greeted the tall red-headed musician with a clap on the arm and a smile.

"How have you been, friend Jiri?"

"Good, Mikal. And you?" Jiri glanced around the house. "Still living in luxury, aren't you? The council would give you a better house if you but asked." Mikal grunted. "It serves its purpose. What would I do with a better house?"

"Spoken like a humble man, Mikal. And that is why I like you. Eva sends her regards and would like to know if you would come by and share a meal with us some evening. She thought that she might invite her cousin . . ."

Mikal threw his head back and laughed. "Don't tell me that Eva is planning on getting into the matchmaking business. I get quite enough of that from others, thank you."

"Ah, well, I told her it wouldn't work. But she wouldn't listen. You know how wives are."

Mikal's laugh faded. "Yes. I know."

Jiri cleared his throat. "Perhaps it is just as well then that I did not come here merely to extend Eva's invitation. I have written a piece of music for you. For The

Festival of the King Stag's Moon if it is not too late." "Never too late. Let us hear it."

Jiri gave a sly smile as he pulled his recorder from his belt. "I thought you might say that. I saw your practice this morning."

"You were there?"

"Watched every step and heard every word." Jiri nodded and pointed to the chair Mikal had just vacated. "Sit. Listen. I think you will like this piece of music."

He put the recorder to his lips, took a breath, and stopped. "It tells of the death of King Stag. How he is hunted by humans and by Death himself. How he sacrifices himself for the forwarding of the seasons and of life. And then..." Jiri's voice trailed off.

"And then what?"

"I do not have the words to say, Mikal. The music will tell you."

"So play it."

Again, Jiri put the recorder to his mouth, then dropped it a second time. "You will, of course, have to imagine the drum and the violin parts. I have friends at the university who would be willing to play, for the standard fee."

Mikal waved his hand impatiently. "Of course. Now play."

After the first few notes, he looked beyond Jiri into the center of the room. His daughter had reappeared and, seen only by him, had begun to dance. He watched, fascinated. Letni never danced, at least not anywhere he had been present to see. Everything that Jiri played she danced; she was the hunter, she was King Stag, she was even Death himself. She danced the end of summer and the cold loneliness of winter, danced it so well that Mikal felt the chill and shivered as he sat. Her physical attributes shifted as he watched, becoming forms of women he had known: his wife, his sisters and his mother; each blending into the other and into her so that the change was hard to recognize. Then Letni grew old in the dance, and Mikal saw the long stringy grey hair and gaunt skeletal face that haunted his dreams.

Just when he felt he could stand no more, the music changed. From the chords of sadness and death, Jiri's music moved into another realm, a realm of hope and love and rebirth. And Letni changed again, the hair that whirled around her dancing form becoming lustrous and healthy, curling about a body that was not Letni's, was not one he had ever seen before. In this form she danced the last few bars, before fading entirely from his sight.

"Is it possible?" Mikal whispered. Jiri finished playing, and, following Mikal's glance, he turned around to stare at the empty room. Mikal shook his head again; this time the wetness on his face came from tears.

"Is what possible?"

Mikal started as if waking from a dream. Perhaps it was just a dream, he thought.

"Did you not see her? I thought perhaps since your music drew her..."

"Who are you talking about?"

"My daughter, Letni."

Jiri looked around uneasily. "I have never seen your daughter, Mikal. I did not know that you had one."

"I do." He paused, got up from the table and walked to the center of the room, searching for her presence. She was not there. Mikal kept his voice pitched low. "Or rather, I had one, once. She died years ago."

"And her ghost was here? Nothing so unusual about that, Mikal, this is Morobrany, after all. Where one may die and never depart, held permanently in Death's evil thrall without hope of redemption."

"Those words are heresy, Jiri. One should be careful of voicing them."

Jiri laughed. "One should be especially careful of shouting similar sentiment in the town's square for all to hear. But here it is just you and I. And your daughter,

I suppose. Letni was her name?" Mikal nodded.

"A lovely name."

"She is, or was, a lovely child."

"And her ghost's presence disturbs you?"

"Her ghost does not belong here!" Mikal exploded into anger. "She has no place in Morobrany's worship of Death. She died very far away."

"Then why is she here?"

"She is my reward." Mikal spoke the last word with clenched teeth and fists. "For being a good and faithful servant of Death."

Jiri cleared his throat nervously. "We all serve in our ways. One can play the music and dance the dance without bowing low. Your festivals . . ."

"I was not referring to my work, Jiri. That is, at least, a clean and honest duty, providing a service and an outlet to the people of this town. But I have performed other deeds, unspeakable deeds, for which I can not and should not be forgiven."

"Life causes us all to do cruel things, Mikal. And Death foists even more cruelty upon us. I know you.

You are a good man."

"You do not know."

"How can I know, if you will not tell me?"

"Then I will tell you." He looked around the house for a trace of Letni.

"Is she here now?"

"I do not know. She is good at hiding, she always says. Perhaps it does not matter. Perhaps it is time she knew the kind of man her father is.

"Poor little thing she never really knew her mother. And I was not much of a substitute, traveling as I did from town to town, performing and learning. It never seemed proper to bring the girl with me so she would stay behind, mostly in the care of my mother, who was old and crippled. Not a good life for a little girl, but I was too proud to ask for help in raising my daughter. I should have been a different man. I see that now."

Jiri nodded. "It is always easier to look back on the road traveled and see the path you should have taken."

"True. And more truth is that I loved the girl. Perhaps I loved her too much. But she was all I had.

"Our village was remote, you understand. Despite the fact that The Plague had ravaged most of the surrounding area, we had remained free. We were blessed, and some of the more prideful of us, myself foremost among them, felt we were invincible. Then one day, when I was returning from a festival in a town far into the mountains, I met a woman sitting at the side of the road. She was very sick, I could see her tremble with the fever even huddled as she was into a thin blanket. I walked up to her, my shadow fell over her and she looked up. The blanket fell back and I thought for a moment 'here is the face of death' — the thin blistered skin stretched tightly over white bones, the grey hair, falling in strings over a wasted body.

"'Approach me not, young man,' she said. 'Just go your way and leave me to die.'

"But I could not. In what I thought was an act of kindness, I gave her water from my flask, food from my pack, added my cloak to her blanket to give her warmth."

"But certainly those were all acts of kindness, Mikal." "I know now that kindness was not in my heart, Jiri. Pride was there: the idea that I had power and that I was pure enough to remain untouched by sickness.

"Whatever my reasons, I comforted the woman as best as I could. 'Stay here,' I said to her, 'I will fix you a place to lie down and when you feel strong enough, I will help you back to my village so that you can recover.'

"'No, she said in horror, 'you must not.' But I was not to be discouraged and walked away to collect brush to make her a bed, no easy task, since it was late in winter. When I returned, she was gone. How she could have disappeared so quickly as sick as she was I never will understand. I searched for her, but finding nothing, I picked up my cloak from where she'd left it and continued on to my village."

Mikal stared off into empty air for a short time, picturing in his mind the old woman, remember how Letni had transformed in the dance. He passed his hand over his eyes, to attempt to remove the image. "The day after I arrived home, people began to sicken. And die. They all died, one after the other, while I alone remained healthy. The last to go was Letni, my little child of the summer. When she breathed her last tortured breath in my arms, I knew I had killed her, had killed all of them. And that my survival was the cruel gift of Death. I heard him laugh, Jiri. I felt his presence as near to me as you, felt his hand on my shoulder as if he were complimenting me on a job well done."

"And so you came to Morobrany. When did Letni come to you?"

"She'd never left. The morning I left my village she was at my side and has been with me ever since. Perhaps that is why it was so easy to pretend that she is not what she is."

"And now? What will the two of you do now?"

Mikal shook his head. "I have no idea, Jiri. Her presence here is wrong; I have always known that. But I held on to her regardless. Even if Death would permit, even if I could let her go, how do I?"

"There are ways, Mikal. But it would mean you must renounce the worship of Death."

"It is not hard to renounce something one does not believe, Jiri. I do not worship Death."

"Then whom do you worship?"

"I worship no gods. They have all deserted me, leaving me with nothing but the inevitability of Death. That sovereignty is what I acknowledge, nothing more."

"Semantics, my friend. Mere semantics." Jiri walked to the door and smiled. "But we will not quarrel over that now. It may be that I can help. You must resolve in your heart if you will let Letni go, or no. And I will study the problem; a spirit not bound by Death should be redeemable."

"Jiri, I thank you, though I like not being in any man's debt. As repayment I will buy that piece of music from you. And fund the musicians needed."

"You would have done that anyway, Mikal." Jiri laughed, "I knew you wouldn't be able to resist the music. But perhaps it will stand as payment for now. And I will bring the musicians by tomorrow after sunset."

Letni did not appear for the rest of the day. Mikal went about his business, consisting mostly of lessons in dance to the children of the wealthy. The councils' gratitude for his services extended only to his title and his house. Money was needed to pay for food and for the services of musicians.

The house felt strangely empty without Letni's presence. Normally she enjoyed watching the lessons, hiding away in some corner, so as not to be a distraction. Mikal could always hear her, though, laughing quietly about some clumsy mistake. And later, she would sit by the fire and tell him stories she'd made up about the wealthy children and what they did when they weren't tripping over each others' feet.

She showed up after dark. Her eyes looked suspiciously wet and he wanted to comfort her, to hold her in his arms as he often had after her mother's death. Instead he just nodded to her. "Daughter."

"Papa. I'm tired tonight. I don't want to talk. I just want to sleep."

"Sleep then, little one, and dream sweet."

She curled up on his cot, slowly drifting off to sleep, becoming less and less visible, until she could no longer be seen. All that remained to indicate her presence was a slight scent and muffled sobs.

Mikal sat staring at the fire and he heard in his mind the words he had spoken to Jiri. Having Letni around was a reward. For him, at least, giving him the semblance of love and family. But for her? He was never quite sure what she thought of her life or of her non-life, content as he was to perpetuate the lie that they had a normal father-daughter relationship. And she never said the words to contradict him.

"Oh, Letni," he whispered to where she should have been sleeping, "you were always such a joy to me. But you should be free. Death is not the god you should be worshiping."

Quietly he pulled a chair over and slept there for the night, keeping vigil, as he often had before she died.

In the morning she was back, but subdued, and called to him from the cot. "Papa, I was hiding again, yesterday. Did you wonder where I was?"

Mikal gave her a sad smile. "I always wonder where you go, daughter, although I do not ask, and you do not tell. But you should know that you need never hide, I am not ashamed of you."

"Most of the time when I am hiding I am right here. In this house, with you. I was here all day yesterday. I heard the story you told the musician. It seemed familiar to me, so familiar. But the end was frightening. I don't remember the end like that." She stopped talking, got out of the bed and slowly glided across the room toward him, her feet never touching the floor. For the first time since she'd died, she was acting like what she was.

It seemed to take her forever to reach Mikal, but when she did she looked straight up at him, locking her eyes onto his. "Papa, tell me the truth. Am I a ghost?"

"Letni," Mikal began and discovered that he could not find the words to say. But he knew that she saw the answer in his eyes. Nothing in his life had prepared him for this moment; he had spent years trying to deny how she had died, writhing in pain and fever while he stood by helpless. So he had welcomed and treated her ghost as what he most wanted: a normal child, alive and thriving.

She could never be that. Never again. And with that painful knowledge, he felt he had killed her for a second time.

He looked into the eyes of his daughter, once so trusting and open, now flooded with suspicion and fear. And said the hardest words he had ever said. "Yes, little one, you are a ghost. You have been dead for over five years."

"Oh, Papa." She burst into tears, faded and was gone.

Mikal went through his day woodenly, distracted.

The dance lessons seemed interminably longer than normal, the students more clumsy and inane. When he was alone he would call to Letni repeatedly. There was no answer, although he could feel her presence, just beyond his senses. It was maddening.

Over and over again he attempted to contact her, searching for words to touch her. "I know I have hurt you, daughter, and hurt you deeply. But you must know that I love you. That you were, no, you are my one joy in life."

He made her promises. "I will find a way to undo all the wrong I have done you."

He scolded and pleaded and cajoled, but she would not appear. As sunset approached, he began to ready the house for Jiri's return visit. "The musicians are coming tonight, Letni," he said as he moved the chairs around the dance area. "You should come and hear them play. And you could dance again. I did not get a chance to tell you, but your dancing was wonderful. I was so proud."

"Papa?"

Just like that, she stood in front of Mikal, pale and thin, eyes reddened and swollen. He nodded. "Yes?"

"I can dance tonight? So that even the others can see me?"

"Please, little one. The time for hiding is past."

The musicians arrived earlier than Jiri. Although Mikal knew them, few words were exchanged other than those of greeting. The easy friendship he shared with Jiri was unusual, most of the townsfolk avoided anything but the most formal contact. His position along with his aloofness and foreignness held him apart, a distance he thought he preferred.

Letni sat by the fire, attired, he realized with a sinking of his heart, in her burial dress. Mikal could tell that the men saw her, but they said nothing. The mugs of apple brandy Mikal offered were politely declined.

But when Jiri entered, the mood lightened. He greeted everyone warmly and walked to where the little girl sat. He leaned over and smiled. "And you must be Letni. It is an honor to meet you."

She nodded and smiled shyly, unused to contact with anyone other than Mikal. He reached down to touch her head, his hand went right through her. Trying to hide his surprise, he shrugged, then winked at her. "So, let's get started, shall we?" Jiri rubbed his hands together and joined the other musicians. "Just an initial rehearsal, so Mikal can hear it the way it was meant to be heard."

Jiri was right, the music, fine though it was the other night, was greatly improved by the addition of the other instruments. Mikal sat next to Letni and listened. Halfway through she leaned over to him and whispered.

"Will this music help me go home?"

"Do you want to go, daughter?"

"Yes, now that I know that I am a ghost." She choked over the word a little. "I do not belong here, you have often said that. I should move forward. But I do not want to leave you alone."

"I know. And I do not want you to leave. But..."

She nodded. "I think I must go. The music pulls me, Papa."

Mikal said nothing, but nodded and both of them turned their attention back to the musicians.

The last note lingered and echoed for a long time. Mikal stood up and clapped his hands together. "Excellent," he said, "excellent. Now there is a piece of music to make even King Stag proud. Shall we do it again? And this time Letni and I will dance."

Hours later, Mikal motioned for a stop. "That is enough for now, I think. Shall we meet for rehearsal tomorrow at the same time?"

The other musicians agreed and accepted a mug or two of apple brandy before they left. Jiri lingered; he and Mikal sat at the table and Letni came over to them. "Thank you, Jiri," she said sincerely. "It is good music to dance to."

"And you dance very well, my lady. Now you should rest."

Obediently, she slipped into the cot, settled under the covers and faded away.

"I can see why you cannot let her go, Mikal. She is a beautiful child."

"But I must let her go, Jiri. It is time. It is past time. And she wishes to go." He drained his mug and poured himself another. "If only I knew how to say goodbye."

"I have some thoughts," Jiri said, "for how to set her free. It may not work, but if she were mine, I would try." His voice grew softer. "There are rites, older than the worship of Death, to ensure the entrance of the soul to heaven. I thought to embed these rites into the music and perform it on the night of the festival. Death will be too busy, perhaps, accepting the worship of the people, to notice what we do."

"And why would you take this risk for me, Jiri?"

"Because you are my friend, Mikal, and because I must."

"Is there danger for the child? I do not want her harmed."

Jiri shook his head slowly, "There is always a danger. My hope is that for her it will be small. That either her spirit will depart in peace, or that it will remain, in which case she is no worse off than now. Death should not have the power to harm an innocent soul."

"Then let us do as you plan. And thank you."

They began rehearsals in earnest the following day. After much discussion it was decided that the extra parts of the rites would be only performed the evening of the festival. And would be kept secret between Mikal and Jiri. The other musicians would no doubt notice the additions, but would be innocent of the plot.

The day of the festival finally arrived; a cold but clear autumn morning. Both Mikal and Letni were quiet, nervous about what that night would bring for them. She faded in and out of sight, practicing some of the more difficult steps and transformations and Mikal watched, offering some guidance, but content merely to see her and be with her.

Late in the afternoon, she stopped. "Papa?"

"Yes?"

"I'm ready. I'm ready for all of it."

"That is good, daughter. And you are sure you want to do this?"

"I am sure." Her voice was quiet, more mature than he had ever heard before. "It is time for me. You know that. And something is whispering deep inside of me that it is time for you, as well."

"Ah, Letni-cas, but it will be hard to let you go."

"You must let me go."

Mikal stooped down close to her, wanting nothing more than to take her in his arms and hold her close to him as he used to. Instead he closed his eyes and remembered the precious scent of her hair and the feel of her little arms clasped tight around his throat. It would have to be enough, he realized, to last him the rest of his life.

But when he opened his eyes again, she was holding him although he could not feel the embrace. Then again, he thought, perhaps I did feel her after all. And he smiled.

By the time Mikal and Letni arrived at the town square the musicians were already in place, entertaining the rather restless crowd with incidental music. She was again appropriately clad in her burial garment, although that would change with her as she danced. He wore dun-colored leather breeches and tunic, the skin of the stag as was required. Around his wrists were bracelets of bells, an aid to the dancing and an aid to the rite of Letni's passage. Mikal saw that most of the men had brought flasks and antlers, hoping for the typical drunken debauchery. He shook his head slowly as he walked to the center of the square. "Not during my festival," he muttered. Then he turned around slowly, his arms outspread, twitching his wrists to ring the bells and call the townsfolk to attention. "People of Morobrany," he spoke the traditional words, slowly and pitched lower than normal, so that all would have to stop their speaking and listen, "Tonight we gather to dance the Moon of King Stag. Ruler of the wild woods and mountains, yet he gives his life so that you and your children may eat and be clothed." Mikal paused, hesitating to speak the words he knew had been added to the festival 50 years ago. But before the audience could notice, he continued. "Mighty though he is, witness here how even King Stag is subservient to the master, Death."

He nodded to the musicians and the drums began. Mikal stepped to one side, rang the bells, and gestured first with one arm to the full harvest moon above them. It was ringed with orange, a favorable omen, and the audience gave a low sigh. Then he pulled his arm down and with palm outstretched he beckoned to the center of the square. Letni appeared suddenly to the astonishment of the people;

she stepped lightly and delicately, placing her feet carefully as if she were walking in the deep forest. Then she lifted her head and scented the air and in an instance became King Stag. Tall, magnificent and beautiful.

The audience gasped when they realized that this was not a stage trick, but that the girl who danced for them this evening was a ghost. Mikal heard a discordant note come from the musicians and glanced at Jiri, who only smiled and nodded. The rite had begun.

Mikal removed the mask of Death that had been secured to his belt. Holding it up in the air, he turned again, so that all could see it. As King Stag, Letni sensed Death and pranced in alarm, her front hoofs thrusting into the air and pounding again to the ground. Mikal hunched down, allowing the crowd to feel her panic and her anger, wishing as he did so that they had secured a few more dancers to take on the roles of Death's hunters. But when he donned the mask and stood back up, striking a threatening pose, he noticed five or six wispy figures materializing around him.

The audience gasped again, although not as surprised as they had been by Letni's initial appearance. Mikal hesitated again, wondering if these spirits had been called by the ritual or the festival or merely came to give honor one of their own. He took another quick glance at Jiri who shrugged and kept playing. The dance must continue, Mikal thought, and hoped the other ghosts knew their parts.

They did. And the dance continued. As the music spoke of death and winter, the hunt, the ultimate hunt, prolonged and painful, played before a spellbound audience. King Stag was proud, brave and resourceful in fending off attack, but he was growing tired and the hunters were not mortal. The ending was inevitable. They hounded and harried him until he stood, presumably blocked into a blind canyon. He was flecked with sweat and steam came from his nostrils as he continued to fight, flailing out with his hooves and his antlers at the dead hunters. One by one they fell before him and disappeared until only Death was left.

Mikal stood in front of Letni and felt tears begin to stream down his face under the mask of Death. She had been flickering in and out of vision during the last minutes of the dance. The ritual was working. It was time to say goodbye.

Death raised his sword and his eyes met those of King Stag. He struck, the creature fell to his knees and collapsed to the ground. Mikal raised his hands, ringing the bells on his wrists and gave Death's victory shout.

At that moment, the music changed as it always had during rehearsal. But this time it seemed to Mikal that the themes of rebirth and hope had deepened. He tore off the mask of Death and threw it onto the stones of the square, crushing it under his feet. Mikal dropped to the ground next to the fading figure of the stag; gently he moved the head so that it rested in his lap. Bending down, he kissed, not the head of the animal, but the head of his daughter. And for one brief second he could actually feel her, she had form and substance.

Letni smiled at him. "Papa," she said.

And then she was gone.

Afterwards there was silence. And the townspeople went their way, quiet and subdued, even those who had come bearing drink and antlers, until at last only Jiri and Mikal remained.

Jiri gave Mikal a brief embrace. "That was quite a show, my friend. How will you top it next year?"

Mikal shook his head. "I do not know. Perhaps I won't even try."

"And Letni?"

"She is at peace. Thank you."

"And Death did not even put up a fight!" Jiri clapped Mikal on the shoulder. "And those other dancers? I think we may have sent a few more souls along their way." He chuckled, "And so, should I be on my way to Eva now. You know how she worries. Good night." "Good night."

Mikal walked away, then looked back for a moment to the dance floor where he had last seen his daughter.

"Good night, Letni-cas," he whispered, "Dream sweet."

Clouds covered the full moon now and the square seemed dark and distant. But in the shadows, Mikal saw a dark figure stoop over, pick up the torn mask of Death and put it on. The man stood, laughed, gave a wide sweeping bow, faded away.

Mikal shivered and hurried home.

*Written for a collection of vampire poetry that never happened. Like all poetry, I think this works best when read out loud.*

## THE DEBT

Eyes, dark as night, seek mine across the room
Closer now and smaller.
Contact made,
I am torn away from me.
You brush my shoulder, you whisper my name.
A low laugh calls to me,
Compels my obedience at your side.
Alone now, no time for words, but for tears,
A touch implies promise,
A debt incurred through all eternity.
And each kiss becomes a crystalline bead
Dropping from your cold lips.
The glinting strand snakes deep within my veins.
Ah, my love, if this need were just the blood,
It could be forgiven.
Survival is pure, your hunger is truth.
But there is more, for you feed, you grow strong,
And knowledge taints the night
With malice.
The clasp breaks, the necklace falls.
Beads of blood shatter, dissolve into ash
Under your feet I die.

*This one sold to Horrors! 365 Stories. It is a companion story (of sorts) to One Green Candle, but had the advantage of being a little more acceptable to a group of male editors. I also feel it is one of my more "Twilight Zone"-ish attempts.*

## FOREVER

"You don't want to do this, John." Susan looked up at him from where she'd been sitting, filing her nails. He can't leave, she thought, I won't let him. She put down the emery board and watched him pace the room, listening unmoved while he blurted out his sad, pathetic tale of lost love and life. "You really don't want to do this."

"Susan," he crossed the room, taking one of her hands in his, "I don't want to hurt you, but I have never wanted anything more in my life."

"Never?" An amused tone crept into her voice. She remembered a time when he'd said that about her, when he'd arrived at the door of this apartment, flushed and trembling with passion and love; remembered how easily she'd seduced him away from wife and children so she could enjoy the touch of his hands and the coiled muscles of his arms.

John stammered slightly under her steady gaze. "Th-things have changed, Susan. That's the way of the world. The kids need me; I need them. I have to go back."

Smiling, she rose and wrapped her arms around his neck, kissing the spot behind his ear that always made him shiver. "Well," she whispered, her voice low and seductive, "If you have to go, then go. But leave me something to remember you by."

Susan feigned sleep while he packed his bag, deepening her breathing as he leaned over and kissed her cheek softly. "This is for the best, Susan, you know it is." When she didn't respond to his whisper, he sighed and walked out of the room.

She lay still until she heard the front door close. Then she stretched, sat up in bed and smiled. "'For the best.'" She mimicked his statement, laughing. "All the same, John, you *don't* want to do this. And you *will* be back."

She hurried to the bathroom to collect what he'd left her. And as she worked she ticked off the ingredients in her mind: hair, fluids, skin cells, blood — all gathered from her body and her sharpened nails and placed in a paper cup.

Without bothering to dress, Susan went to the kitchen. "Much simpler to make than the last candle," she said as she prepared the wax and the mold. "And given the quality of the 'remembrances,'" she purred the word, "it should be much more effective." Obviously, she thought as she worked, the one she'd prepared to bring John to her had been weak, mostly because she'd had to use shoddy materials: hair from his head, sweat from the headband she'd stolen from his gym bag the night they'd met; enough to bring him, but not strong enough to keep him.

"This time," she removed the candle from the mold and set it on the counter. "This time, John, it will be forever." She lit the wick. The flame sputtered, then flared up, burning steady and strong. Susan sat cross-legged on the floor, rocking back and forth, humming a tuneless song, her eyes focused on the candle until all that remained was the fire, the man and one word.

"Forever."

Hours later when the candle was just a pool of melted wax and carbon two distinct sounds woke her from her trance: a scraping of a key in the front door and the ringing of the phone. Susan gave a smug smile and got up from the floor. John was back, forever. She knew it. Gone would be all thoughts of wife and children; she would be the only one he ever wanted.

Turning her back to the opening door, she answered the phone.

"Ms. Black?" The urgent voice sent a small chill through her.

"Speaking."

The caller cleared his throat. "You are listed as the contact for John Turner, is that correct?"

"Yes, he lives here."

"Ah." There was a pause. Susan heard the front door shut. "There's been an automobile accident. And I'm sorry to tell you that Mr. Turner didn't . . ."

"Didn't what? Didn't stop?"

Only half listening to the call, Susan smiled at the familiar feel of John's body pressed behind her. His hands caressed her shoulders, but they were unusually cold and clammy. She gasped, dropping the phone, staring at the sticky blood dripping onto her breasts.

As if from a long distance she heard a voice say "… no, he didn't survive."

The voice in her ear was much closer and clearer. "Forever," it rasped. "Forever."

*Written for Brain Box I, this was accompanied by the following non-fiction piece describing the thinking process behind the story.*

*I seem to come up with some of my most fertile ideas while traveling. This story is no exception. Several years ago I was in Las Vegas for an HWA weekend. It was the first time I had ever been that far from home and family and I looked forward to the vacation. So much so that I had deliberately scheduled my return flight for a day or two after the weekend's events were done. What I hadn't realized was that Vegas is only a wonderful place to be when you have money and friends. After all the quarters have disappeared into the slots and the video poker machines, after all the friends and acquaintances leave, Vegas is a desperate and lonely place. By the time Monday arrived I was alone and had lost most of the money I'd brought with me. I had expected to lose it, of course, but still somewhere deep inside I had hoped for one big win and the freedom that would grant me.*

*I sat in a restaurant in the casino and ordered a cup of coffee and an English muffin. As I ate, I did what every writer does. I watched the people, concentrating mostly on one particular man. He emptied his pockets onto the counter and began to count his change, over and over again. Here was someone who'd lost even more than I had and I could almost feel his desperation from across the room. He was a man consumed by that place, as if he'd been eaten away from the inside by some strange and horrible disease.*

*I checked out of the hotel almost immediately and despite the fact that I had about eight hours before my flight, I caught the shuttle to the airport so that I could escape from the awful emptiness of the man in the restaurant.*

*But even as I sat in the airport bar with a huge glass of beer in front of me, I couldn't get the image of the broken man out of my mind.*

*So I opened my briefcase, took out my yellow tablet and began to write him a story.*


## FREEDOM


The clinic is white and chrome with a medicinal smell that clings to my throat and stings my eyes. It has no heart and no life, despite the fact that whole families have lived here, babies have been born here, tears have been cried, voices have been raised in joy and anger. It is sterile and they keep the halls and rooms spotlessly clean, as if simple purity could make up for what is lacking. But what is missing is so huge and necessary that even the children sense the lack; their play is rougher, their hugs tighter. Surely, I think, as I endure the pressure of their arms around my throat, surely there was a time when little ones did not need to cling so desperately to warmth and affection. A time when they could let go without fear.

I can remember that time, when the two worst diseases were cancer and AIDS. It was before the great plague of '08 that left millions of rotting corpses in New York City, the flesh literally oozing off their bones as they melted in the once crowded streets. Before the even more feared sickness that became rampant a few years later — the one that left the body clean and untainted, only to corrupt and distort the human thinking process. Before the zombies, as the first were called, and the loons, the second. Before the clinics were established.

We had been on vacation when the first plague hit — showing our four-year-old daughter the wonders of the Grand Canyon and the west coast — never realizing how that trip would change our lives. Missy had been tucked safely in her hotel room bed; John and

I had watched the news, first in sleepy complacency, then with skepticism, and finally in a horrified silence that must have blanketed the entire world. Our second child was conceived that night, the result of a quick, furtive coupling on the cool tile of the bathroom floor, one last attempt to deny the irrefutable facts of the television screen, to block out the vision of the death throes of millions of people, a reaffirmation of life. A foolish act, perhaps, but here he comes, bursting into my presence, my littlest one, John Michael Daniels, Jr. with news for me.

"Mommy!" His face is flushed in exertion, he must have run at top speed, I think, through the sealed tube that connects our dwelling with his schoolroom.

"Guess what?" He flings himself into my arms and I return his embrace, relishing the feel of his frantic breath on my neck.

"What's up, sweetie?" I kiss the top of his head and brush back a lock of hair.

"Billy's gettin' out! And his whole family, too. We had a good-bye party at school today. And guess what?" He moves out of my arms, a happy smile on his face. Missy does not return from school until later and he's always thrilled to be the first one to bear good tidings. "We had cupcakes in the slot. And balloons, too." His expression falls a bit. "But mine broke."

"I'm sorry, Johnny."

"That's okay." He gives a typical boyish shrug, then he smiles again. "But guess what? Billy's balloon broke too. Only he cried."

"Well," I say, the font of motherly wisdom, "I don't think that's because of the balloon. It's probably because he doesn't want to leave his friends behind."

"Yeah," Johnny agrees reluctantly. I see in his eyes many unasked questions about the release of Billy's family, but decide to allow him to ask them in his own way and time. "Anyway, Miss Jenkins said that there'd be another cupcake when we get home. Can I have it now?"

"Sure, honey. It's a while before dinner."

Johnny gives me a questioning look. "Mom?"

"Yeah?"

"Do you think that . . ."

"What?"

"Oh, never mind. Will Missy have a cupcake, too? Or should I save her half of mine?"

I reach over and tousle his hair. "I think Missy should have one, Billy's brother is in her class. So you can eat yours now and she'll have hers later."

"Great." Johnny goes to the food slot, claims his prize and settles down in front of the TV.

Much later, after the arrival of our evening meal, after the studies are completed, after Missy and Johnny are finally asleep, the excitement of the day forgotten, I place an audio-only call to Billy's mother.

"Hi, Sarah," I say when she answers, "I just wanted to say goodbye and good luck."

The silence on the other end of the phone is tense at first. "Annie," she finally says, "I was going to call before I left. Honest."

I laugh uneasily. Too many of the people I knew as friends had left without that call. "I know, Sarah," I say reassuringly, "but I thought you'd be busy, getting ready to leave . . ."

"Yeah, I am, sort of." Her voice holds all sorts of unspoken thoughts and emotions. As does mine. After all, she and her family were leaving and I and mine were to be left behind. "Tom called."

"That's great, Sarah."

"Yeah," her tone is dry, "he's meeting us at the front gates." "That'll be nice."

"I guess," she says reluctantly, then quickly, "I mean, it'll be good to see him, and all, but we've been here so long, and he's been out there . . ." Sarah's voice trails away.

She pauses while we both consider the possibilities of 'out there.'

"I'm sure it will work out."

"Yeah. He sounds good, though. Better than I'd expected."

Suddenly there's nothing left to say and another awkward silence ensues. Sarah breaks it first. "See you," the note of finality in her voice belying her standard goodbye. "You take care."

The connection is broken and as the tears fall down my face I'm relieved that I'd done without the video reception.

I can't sleep, not a new development. I seldom sleep these days. The bed is empty and cold. Over and over in my mind, I envision the meeting of Sarah and Tom at the clinic's front gate: the tears and the joy, a bittersweet reunion. Would she find him changed, a stranger or would she know him instantly and fly into his arms, as desperate as the children for the warmth of touch? Punching down the pillow for what seems the hundredth time, I roll over and sign, reliving unwillingly the parting of our family, our separation and alienation from one another.

We had been driving through the desert, when we hit the first medical emergency road block. I'm still not sure where we'd hoped to go, how we thought we'd escape the plagues, the final indignity of no control over our bodies and our lives. I think that John just kept driving because that was all that he could think to do.

Twenty four hours later, the testing done, I had waited, nervous and tearful, in an isolated room. Escorted by an enviro-suited medic,

Missy finally joined me and clutched at my hand, restless and uncertain.

"Mommy?" Missy whined. "What's happening? Where's Daddy?"

"I don't know, angel," I lied to her, having already discussed the alternatives with the medical staff, having been convinced by the detection of the new life I carried to agree to our admission to one of the newly established health centers, the clinics.

"Hope, Mrs. Daniels," the anonymous masked and suited doctor had said, "that is what you carry inside you, hope, and that's why you and your daughter must come with us.

But hope died inside me when John appeared in the adjacent room, his face stricken and pained. Separated by much more than a thick panel of glass, only our eyes could meet. Then he was led away and Missy and I were taken to the clinic. From that day up through the next six years I existed only for the children, not possessing any life of my own, nor desiring one.

At breakfast, Johnny's questions from the previous day surface.

"Mommy?" He breaks the seal on his cereal package and the aroma of hot oatmeal pervades the room.

"Yes, dear?" My voice is muffled and slightly absent, as I am occupied in braiding Missy's hair, an elastic band clutched between my teeth.

"What's it like outside?"

"Well, Johnny..." I begin, but Missy interrupts.

"I told you, dork head," she winces a little as I pull slightly harder on her hair than I need to, but with the confidence of a ten-year-old she continues undaunted. "It's hot and sandy and ugly. But the sky is so blue. And," she pauses a minute, her voice growing wistful, "Daddy's there, waiting for us."

"Do you think we can go soon, Mommy? Billy says he's going to climb a real-live tree and lie down in the grass and go to a park and everything." Johnny gives me a sidelong glance, "Could you ask the doctors if they'll let us go? We'll be good, I promise."

I finish tightening the band around Missy's braid and turn her head from side to side, checking on the evenness of her hair, glancing intently at the exposed area of skin behind each of her ears.

And in that glance, the hope that had been dead for six years is resurrected and I smile through my tears.

"Why not?" I agree. "I'll ask the doctors today and we'll see them right after school."

"There can be no doubt about the prognosis, Mrs. Daniel," the doctor explains, "you and your family will be leaving the clinic the day after tomorrow."

"All of us?" My voice quavers, all three of us was more than I'd hoped for.

"Yes, all three of you. Please make whatever arrangements you need to. Departure time is eight a.m." He makes a few final notations on our files and closes the folder.

Missy is quiet and thoughtful on the way home; Johnny is boisterous, running ahead of us through the tube, then running back. "Trees," he sings, in a childish chant, "grass, birds and skies." He takes my hands in his, a surprisingly adult gesture. "And freedom, Mommy, freedom. No glass tubes, no food slots, no doctors." Then he drops my hands and runs ahead again, singing of trees and birds and grass. And freedom.

Missy, six years wiser, is still quiet, vaguely disturbed. "Will Daddy be there? Waiting?"

"I hope so, angel." The indecision in my voice causes her to wrinkle her brow.

"Do you think he'll want us now? Do you think he'll know us?"

I can't answer that question, so I hold her close to me, my arm around her waist, as we enter the dwelling that had been our home.

He is waiting, my husband, my children's father. Before our release, the doctors explained that he could not call, like Tom had, but that he would be there to collect his family. And so after our final meal, after the endless medical instruction and release forms, after the calls had been made and the friends wished farewell, we headed down one final tube toward the clinic gates. Our tube, actually an endless warren of isolated hallways, would be sealed off, our living quarters forever more unoccupied. Slowly and surely the population of the clinics was dwindling, as more people attained their freedom.

John knows us and he extends his arms to his family, to the wife and daughter he hasn't seen in six years, and the son he's never seen at all. His smile is as I remember and his eyes are warm.

"Annie," his tone is muffled, the lower half of his face covered in bandages, "I'm so sorry, my dear. God damn it all, it sounds terrible to say it, but I hoped never to see you or the children again. Because that would mean . . ."

I glance at the children and shake my head. "Don't say it, John, I know."

He wraps his bandaged arms around me as firmly as possible and hugs me to him.

Missy looks around her, eyes wide open, and steals over to my side to look up shyly at her father. "Maybe," she whispers, "it's not all that bad out here after all." But I see in her eyes the realization finally of what this all means.

Johnny, too young to understand, is joyful as only a child can be. "Trees," he sings, running in dizzying circles around us. "Trees and birds and sky and grass. Freedom."

"Freedom." I echo his word as I look at the world once again. I watch my little ones standing under the naked sky, drinking the morning sun. All would be perfect, all would be beautiful, except that in the harsh light of day, I see clearly the signs the doctors had confirmed. Those small patches of skin already beginning to soften as the tissue beneath slowly decomposed. Patches like the ones now on me, like the ones that necessitate the bandages on John's arms and neck.

"How long?" John mouths the words.

"They said six, maybe even ten years." I whisper the words and feel their hopelessness. "There is medication that will help a little and perhaps they'll find a cure."

He nods slowly. "Annie, I am so very sorry."

He and I stand and watch our children run. Missy catches her brother's excitement, forgetting everything else but the fact that we are now free.

Six years, maybe ten years for the children. Less most definitely for John. We will live free. And at the last, we will finally have the freedom to die.

*This story is one of only a few of mine told from a male point of view. I had to do it that way, considering it was written for an anthology called Women Writing Science Fiction as Men.*

## A GOOD IDEA AT THE TIME

I studied him as he walked down the street. A likely suspect, I thought, clad in a suit, tie and carrying an expensive briefcase, but with a confused look in his eye, as if he had lost something very important, something crucial to his life. He was right, of course, he had. They all had. But I was the only man alive who knew that for sure.

As he neared, I straightened my clothes and considered my approach. "Excuse me, sir," I said, respectfully – the ones in suits always appreciated respect. "May I speak with you for a moment? It is a matter of some importance to me. And may be of interest to you."

While he appraised me, I thought of what he must be seeing: an older man, mid to late sixties, dressed normally if shabbily, with a corpulent look that hinted of a not so perfect past. The eyes were sad, but clear, with no trace of possible violence or drugs. In short, I did not look like a mugger or a bum.

He gave me a wary nod.

"For the modest price of a beer and a hamburger, I'll tell you a good story. Yes, I know, it's a line you hear every day in this part of town, but surely you can tell from the way I speak that I'm not one of your usual street scum. I am a highly educated, some might say overeducated, scientist. Once renowned for my discovery of time travel."

This line usually grabbed them or lost them.

"Time travel?" he mused, "I don't remember reading about that in the papers. But you're right, it could be interesting."

Got him. Odd, it usually took more than that, I'd had the whole spiel prepared. Some of my best lines were in that spiel. I was especially fond of: this story also involves the fall of a great mind, a great career and a great civilization. Certainly, good sir, you must agree that is worth the cost of lunch and a beer or two?

As a scientist, though, I'd learned economy of effort. Why waste the words if I already had him hooked.

We entered a bar about a block away. They knew me here, always kept the best booth open for me. I figured it was the least they could do.

"Did you know," I said to him, after we'd been seated and our orders had been taken, "this is the first bar I ever frequented, and the one I always come back to? No, how could you? Still, I've found that there's nothing like a comfortable, straightforward bar, one in which you can drink in silence or in companionship with others of your kind. Mankind, I mean. Notice there are no women in here? That is, to me, part of its charm."

He obliged me by looking around and nodded.

"Not that I don't like women, you understand," I continued, "but every so often a man needs to get away and relax. This sort of bar affords one that luxury."

"Yeah," he smiled, "I know exactly what you mean."

"Even the food here is basic, good food. None of your frills or fads. One of the city magazines voted this place the best hamburger for several years in a row. And they weren't lying. Just wait; you'll be able to see for yourself."

"Actually," he said, his voice slow and reasonable, "I've eaten here before myself. I may even have seen you once or twice, you certainly look familiar. Funny how that works, isn't it?" He paused, then held out his hand. "The name's John Jones. You?"

"Dr. William Jones."

He laughed. "Small world."

"Smaller than you think, Mr. Jones. But in fact it is quite a common name.

"True enough, Doctor. You did say Doctor, didn't you?" He raised an eyebrow, staring pointedly at my clean but ill-fitting, old clothes.

"Yes, I have earned the title of Doctor. It's part of the story, Mr. Jones, all part of the story. But," I saw the waiter approaching with our lunch, "let's eat first, shall we?"

The waiter set our plates down in front of us. "Can I get you anything else, Dr. Jones?"

"Another beer for me, Jim." I looked over at my companion. "You?"

"Sure," he said, "why the hell not?"

The waiter left to draw our beers; I held my plate up in front of my face, sniffed and gave a satisfied sigh. "Ah," I said to Mr. Jones, "look at this. Just the right amount of grease in these, don't you think? See that little pool of it? And then there's the good red meat, medium rare, with lettuce, tomatoes, a nice thick slab of red onion, smeared with real mayonnaise, and topped with a huge slice of melted cheese. They even toast the buns on the grill. A man's meal."

I took a huge bite, grease ran out of the side of my mouth and dribbled down my chin. Wiping it off with my napkin, I smiled. "Have you ever been a vegetarian, Mr. Jones? Do you know what it's like to go years, decades even without ever getting something good to eat?"

"Can't say that I do, Dr. Jones. Why do you ask?"

I shook my head. "Let's finish these first and I'll tell you everything."

The two of us ate in relative silence, interrupted only by the solid sound of chewing.

"Nothing like this," I said before taking that last bite, "nothing else in the world."

He nodded. "Yeah, it's good."

I finished the burger, belched and tapped my chest with my fist. "Pardon me. As much as I love the food, it always makes me burp. But this is a man's bar and no one cares. One is not ostracized for demonstrating basic human actions."

I drained my beer and motioned to Jim to bring another. When he brought it, I took another long drink, wiped my mouth with the back of my hand.

"Here one is not ostracized for basic human actions," I repeated, "but it was not always this way. Or maybe it was. Time has become a difficult subject for me. Is it now? Is it then? I am the only one who remembers."

I paused. Dramatically. "You see, Mr. Jones, I remember the future."

He gave a little snort of disbelief.

I nodded. "Of course you don't believe me, what sane man would? I assure you, though, the story is true. The future I remember is a very clean place, sterile. There are no diseases, no wars, no dissension. Utopia, in other words. Men judge others based on their intellect, on their contribution to society. Children seek to further their education; one needs to coax them to play, to entice them away from their books and their studies.

On a normal day, I would awaken, shower, dress, enter the kitchen to a machine-prepared breakfast of nutrobars and energy drinks. My wife would smile at me, perhaps even kiss me on the cheek, her hair, skin and figure perfectly suited to mine. The rooms of my house were immaculate, no clutter, no dropped crumbs or spilled drinks. Nothing to mar the beauty of the basic but comfortable furniture and the wide expanse of green grass and blue skies visible from the picture windows. The children would be busy with their studies and look up with smiling clean faces if I entered the room."

I grew quiet for a moment at that thought. But continued quickly so as not to lose his attention. "Yes, I have children, or I had them once. They have been swallowed up by another time stream."

I gave him a discerning look. "For all I know, Mr. Jones, you could be my son. In another time and another place."   "Somehow, I doubt that, Dr. Jones."

I chuckled. "Well, to be honest, so do I. But it adds a little bit to the story, I think. The elements of doubt and what if are very important."

Mr. Jones looked at his watch. "About this story, Doctor? Are you going to tell it or not? I have a meeting soon."

I nodded sagely. "Yes, of course, everyone has meetings these days. But they will wait for you, I'm sure."

He gave a non-committal grunt, but stayed in his seat and sipped on his beer.

"Now, we were talking about the future, I believe. It was a very nice place as I remember. I worked in a laboratory outside of Newark, New Jersey as a young man. A very clean and lovely place. Or at least it once was or would be. I haven't been there since the future.

I had everything then. A distinguished career, a loving wife, two daughters and a son on the way. All of it carefully planned and neatly organized. But, when I looked around my gleaming office and my perfect home, I felt that something was missing. Something elemental to the human experience. Disorder, chaos, grit and grime."

"You lived in the utopian future and wanted grime?"

I sighed. "I didn't necessarily think that perfection was the preferred human condition. You see, I was also a historian. And I longed for something that had been lost along the way. Passion, savageness, raw emotion. We knew none of these. And I felt we were lacking because of it."

"So you developed a time machine to better study the past?"

I nodded and gave him the smile that at one time would have been reserved for an especially bright research assistant. "You're quick, Mr. Jones. I'll give you that. I did, indeed, develop a time machine to study the past. It took me years of research, years of experimentation. I could explain the process, but I doubt that you have enough time to hear it all. Or, if you'll pardon me, that you would even have the comprehension necessary for such an explanation. Suffice it to say, I succeeded in creating my machine. I studied the past with avid curiosity. Eventually, though, you can probably guess what happened."

"Watching wasn't enough?"

"Exactly." I beamed at him across the table. "I wanted to experience, wanted to jump right into the life I studied. One fateful morning I kissed my perfect wife and my perfect daughters goodbye and took the plunge."

I paused again, staring into my half-empty mug, until Mr. Jones checked his watch and cleared his throat.

"I really must go soon," he insisted. "I'm already more than half an hour late."

"Trust me, Mr. Jones, you will be missing nothing of importance."

He laughed then. "And you know this, of course, because you are from the future."

"No, I know this because I know what this world is like. No one knows better than I."

"Because of your studies?" Jones lifted his mug to his lips.

"No, I know because I made this world what it is today."

He choked mid-gulp, sputtered a bit, then swallowed hard. And began to laugh again. "Now, I suppose I'm to believe you're god?"

"Your belief doesn't matter, Mr. Jones. Shall I continue?"

"By all means. I want to know how this ends."

I finished the last of my beer. "As for me," I said softly, "I don't care about how the story ends, just that it does."

"Excuse me?"

"Nothing. Now, where was I? Oh, yes, I kissed my family goodbye and embarked on my first trip. The year I arrived was a deliberate choice – about 40 years ago, your time. That decade was particularly rife with what I like to call critical patches. It was a time of change, a time of great experimentation. I felt I would fit right in with the society. Coincidently or not, I ended up here. In this very establishment. It was here I had my very first taste of meat, alcohol and the ambiance of a neighborhood bar. I became intoxicated with more than the beer. Still, on that trip, I did nothing but eat and drink."

A laugh behind me caused us both to jump. "He drank way too much, like now," Jim said, setting two more beers in front of us, "and then just walked off without paying his bill. Or so my dad used to tell me."

I gave Jones a sheepish grin. "I'd left the appropriate currency in my other pair of pants. Or something like that. I believe, though, that I was merely drunk on the life I'd found around me.

It was inevitable that on my return to the future, I found myself dissatisfied. I craved the experiences I'd had in the past. Simple, basic experiences which I felt I deserved. Eating meals with my family became a chore. The healthy food I'd once loved became dry and tasteless, the energy drinks, dull, discussions with my wife and children became a duty rather than enjoyment. All I could think about was juicy burgers, the taste of an ice-cold beer, the ability to just sit and be silent or converse with others who had the same interests as I."

He looked around with a mock-surprised expression. "This is a time-traveler's bar?"

"Now, Mr. Jones, please try to control your sarcastic tendencies. You know what I mean."

He shrugged. "Yeah, I do. Sorry. Go on."

"I would sneak away to the past every opportunity I'd get, merely to come here, to this bar. I would eat and drink and then return to the future, growing more discontented with every trip. My wife accused me of seeing another woman, my children felt that I was ignoring them, I grew careless at work and was threatened with termination. This establishment seemed to be the only place now or then that had people who really understood me, people who took me at face value, who allowed me to be the person that I was. I resented the time I spent in the future, began to hate my life there and long for the past, but I thought that my obligations precluded me from making more than small furtive trips.

Until one night as I was sitting in the reading room of my perfect home, I had a revelation. One I felt was greater than the actual discovery of time travel. I could live both lives. Even with my invention, my thoughts had been foolishly limited by linear thinking. Ridiculous! Was not every second of time at my disposal? Weeks, months, years: they all belonged to me now. I could spend as much time as I wished and still return to the exact moment of departure.

'Yes!' I jumped up from my chair, startling my two daughters as they poured over their schoolwork. They stared at me with blank faces.

'Father?'

I laughed. "Nothing, daughters, go back to your books. I must go to the lab."

I brought nothing with me except a fairly large stack of currency appropriate to the times. I knew enough of future events to parry this amount into a small fortune. And from then on I knew that the world belonged to me. I traveled, I talked, I ate and drank at every opportunity, meeting influential people I'd only read about, meeting seemingly unimportant people who would become the pivotal points of my future society. And then..."

My voice trailed off and I drained my beer.

"You got bored with it all?"

I gave a short laugh. "Not at all, Mr. Jones. Bored? How on earth could I be bored? I lived like a king; I possessed everything I once dreamed of. Women flocked to me, and men as well. I owned mansions on both coasts and a castle or two in Europe, each fully stocked with the food and drink on which I thrived, each fully manned with a staff dedicated to my every need.

I woke exhilarated every morning and went to sleep each night exhausted, but utterly pleased with the day's events. Now this, I thought, is truly Utopia. Full-blooded and meaningful, not thin and ethereal and lifeless like the life I'd left behind in the future."

"So what went wrong?"

I cocked an eyebrow at him. "You're an intelligent man, Mr. Jones. Surely you can figure it out."

He sat silent for a second, thinking. Then, "Aha! All of your interaction with the past began to affect the present."

I nodded. "And worse yet, it began to change the future. Suddenly, I no longer knew what was going to happen. The world became uncharted territory for me. I, the man who conquered time, had been trapped in a world that grew more and more incomprehensible with each passing day. I lost my fortune in disastrous stock ventures, saw each of my mansions sold off, one by one. The women abandoned me, the staff of dedicated employees went elsewhere. Gone was the exhilaration, the excitement. When I woke one morning, penniless and homeless, shivering in an alley, I knew that all I had left was the future I'd abandoned. Tail tucked between my legs, I returned."

Jim brought me another beer. I'd told this story so many times in here to so many different men, he knew exactly where I'd need the comfort. I drank, long gulps, like a drowning man gasping for air.

"And?" my companion prompted me. "And?"

I sighed. Drank. Sighed again. "And, Mr. Jones, there was no future. Not the one I'd left. No wife, no children, no perfect home, no perfect society.

At first I thought that the machine had malfunctioned and returned me to an area of the past I had never visited. The streets were filled with rubble and trash and barely recognizable human remains. This could not be my time; gone were the trees and the broad expanses of grass. The sky hung, dark and sooty, over a landscape that felt right and wrong at the same time. Still, this place was of interest. I wondered when I had ended up.

I explored this new time. Words cannot express the horrors I witnessed there. Plagues, degenerative diseases, insanity. I held myself distant from it all, viewing it dispassionately, like the scientist I once was. For a time."

I stopped and looked him in the eye. "You see, I fought to hold onto the belief that this could not be my perfect future, fought to find the malfunction in the machine. But the evidence was there and could not be denied for long. A scrap of newspaper. A video report flashing on a screen. This, I realized, the enormity of the revelation stabbing in my gut, was my future. Our future.

Wars had been fought while I'd celebrated in the past. Millions of people died in horrible ways while I was watching a baseball game and enjoying a beer."

I shook my head, wiping away a tear of rage and sadness. "Those sad people of the future. Sick, deformed, dying. They never knew what I had stolen from them. From their children. From the entire human race."

Giving a choked laugh, I grasped my mug. "Take all the tyrants of history, Mr. Jones, add them all up and multiply by the number of years we have occupied this earth and still the total would not equal the enormous consequences of my actions. For what? And well you may ask." I picked up the mug, held it in the air. "For this!" I said and slammed it back down to the table, splashing beer over my hands. "And," I pointed to a tray of food being carried out to a waiting table, "for that! I sold out the future of the human race for nothing but a beer and a burger with the guys."

Jones stared at me, unsure whether to laugh or to cry. I knew exactly how he felt. It was all too absurd. Too ridiculous. And unfortunately, too real.

"But," he said, his voice soft, "how does it end? What did you do?"

"I did the only thing possible. I brought myself back to the past, destroyed the machine so that no one else would be tempted to make the same mistakes that I did. Then I searched for a way to make things different.

Every day, I tell this story to a different person, in the hopes that it will serve as a warning. In the hopes that they will believe enough to change the world."

"And?"

I shook my head. "Not yet, Mr. Jones, it hasn't happened yet. I fear it may never happen."

"So." He pushed back his chair, looked around, and motioned to the waiter. "I'll take the bill now, please." He paid and stood up, extending his hand. I shook it. A good handshake, I thought, firm, strong. He'd been a good choice. Maybe...

"It certainly has been interesting, Dr. Jones. Although I'm not sure I believe a single word, you promised a good story and you delivered."

"I'm glad you enjoyed it. It was an honor for me to tell it to you."

"So," he hesitated, "what will you do now?"

"What else can I do? I'll wait out my days here, telling the story over and over to anyone who'll listen, to anyone who'll pick up the tab." I winked at him. "They really are very good hamburgers."

He nodded and left.

Jim came over and cleared the empty beer mugs. I got up, went to the bathroom. All that beer. Afterwards, I washed my hands and stared into the mirror. The tired eyes of an old man stared solidly back at me. "I'm not sure why you keep trying, old man, it never seems to do any good. So many of them and only one of you. This one, though, I have hopes for him. He felt right."

I nodded back at myself, pushed open the door and walked back down the hallway to the bar, pulling up a stool and staring vacantly at the wide-screen TV.

"You okay?" Jim wiped the counter in front of me and set up another beer.

"Fine." When, of course, I was anything but.

"Was he the one?" Jim's voice contained a hint of laughter. He'd always been a skeptic, like his father before him.

"Maybe. We should know fairly soon. Or at least you will." I barked out a humorless laugh. "I probably won't know a thing."

"He seemed like a good man. What will happen to him?"

"To him?" I gave a small shrug. "Nothing, most likely. To his perception, there will be no difference. He was late for his meeting, we know that for a fact, and as a result, missed the chance to be introduced to Carol Smith. She will be on a plane now, going to Chicago, to meet her fiancé, the one she had once jilted for a man she just met. She will be happy and content, I hope, unaware of the life she missed. And Mr. Jones? I feel sure he will meet another woman who takes his fancy. They will marry and have children. Granted, not the same ones he might have had, if he had not taken time from his schedule to buy a crazy old coot a beer and a burger. And, after all, that was the point."

I stopped and sighed. "Things will not be quite the same, you know. I can't promise that the future will be as bright as the one I'd lived in. But it will be different than the one I glimpsed and, more importantly, it will not be of my doing. Not entirely. Not like before."

I shook my head. "I did the best I could, Jim, to make amends. And I will never know if it sufficed. How could I? If I've done the job I set out to do, I won't have existed."

"What?" Jim looked over at me, alarmed. "What do you mean?"

"I liked Mr. Jones, didn't you? Although he is younger than I remember him, he is still a good man. With solid values. Grandma Carol always used to call him a solid man. Thank goodness Grandfather John always had a kind streak, a love for his fellow man, he was always the kind who would go out of his way to help another, even if all it meant was sharing a meal and listening. And he always did enjoy a good story."

I laughed at memories that had never existed, looking down at my hands resting on the counter. Were they not as solid as they had been before? Was it possible I could I see the surface of the bar shimmering through the skin and bones?

"It's all true?" Jim joined me in looking at my hands. I could hear a trace of awe in his voice. I'd been telling the same story for years and he'd never believed until now.

"Yes, it's all true. I sold the birthright of man for a beer and some grilled meat between two pieces of roll."

"And now you're just going to fade away now? Because your grandfather never met your grandmother?"

"I certainly hope so. But before I go," I smiled at him, seeing my reflection waver slightly in the mirror, trying to calculate how much time I had left before present events caught up with the future and the past, rippling the world to a new configuration, "I think I'd like another hamburger, please. One for the road."

*Another poem, written for me. But you might like it too.*

### JANUARY ORANGES

January oranges
may be picked,
If you're careful to choose
out of your reach.
A full half of the crop
will prove no good;
For they are hard and sour
and fight the knife.
Ah, but the rest are sweet
and soft and lush
And yield to the cut
like a lover's kiss.
Yet, there is a bitterness
even here,
Lurking in the bruised pulp,
the mottled peel.
It's the rushing of spring
you could not wait.
The taunt of might have been
Cut down too soon.

*This story being greatly praised by many and appearing on the final*
*ballot for the HWA's Bram Stoker Award for Short Fiction was a huge*
*surprise to me. It was an even bigger surprise when I finally figured*
*out exactly what this story was saying and why the writing of it was*
*so difficult for me. Sometimes even the author doesn't know, until*
*she's hit upside the head with that two-by-four. I've quit reading it at*
*cons, though, since it invariably makes me cry.*

## MEXICAN MOON

They say he cried at my funeral. The news hounds pounced on
the fact and instantly began their foul speculations about a life that
had never previously been tainted with even the slightest tinge of
scandal. I was, after all, America's Favorite Single Mom, both on vid
and off. I can only imagine what a huge shock it must have been to
the stricken family and the six adopted grieving children to have this
strange, dark and sullen man show up at the service uninvited. They
say he scattered dried rose petals in my coffin, planted a passionate
kiss on my cold, dead lips and strode out without a single word,
tears streaming down his face.

Or so they say. He has kept the disks of all the news stories; I
hear them playing on his viewer late at night.

I have never seen the disks. Their viewing is not part of my
programming. And I have never seen him cry, tears seeming even
less a part of his programming than they would be of mine.

Except for the fact that he has programmed me to cry. I now
possess a few elemental human emotions and reactions. I cry, I grow
angry, I laugh. I even feel a form of hunger, when my power source is

low. But I am just an infant, he says, over and over again. And as an infant, I must learn to become the woman I once was.

Often, I think I must be turning over in my grave.

Tonight he paces in his room. I hear the vid player droning; if I concentrate, I can almost make out the words being played. But I am not to concentrate on that. Instead I have an autobiography to scan. Her autobiography. Or more properly, mine, I suppose, since she is dead and I am she.

I try to obey his orders, but halfway through, I turn the viewer off. Although the life she led, one I can almost remember, seems so distant to me and so unreal, it was, at least, a life. Much more, I realize, than I could ever hope to attain. And here, I think, is a new emotion. I know the name for it. Despair. I do not like it.

But he will be pleased that I felt it. Did she feel it? And was he pleased when she did?

Too many question, I think. Not enough answers. Quietly I rise from my chair and pace about my room as he does in his, absently shedding articles of clothing, until I am naked. It doesn't matter, there is no one here to see me. And even if there were, it would make no difference, an artificial creature has no shame.

Pictures of her adorn the walls, each alternated with a mirror. I stare at them, one at a time, studying her face to see where I fit in. All of the photos are publicity stills from the vid show. All but one. In this one she looks totally different from the polished image the others show. She stands in the middle of the Mexican desert, barefoot and disheveled, golden-tipped hair blown about in the wind, her arm extended toward the camera. It is night in the picture and a moon rises behind her, shining through her thin dress. The light makes her look as if she is glowing from within. Or perhaps it is not a trick of the light. She is beautiful. She is, I realize with a shock, deeply in love.

I study her face. My face. Have I ever smiled like this, a smile as full and rich as the moon behind her? Attempting to imitate it, I peer at her picture, then the mirror, then the picture again. Shaking my head, I stop trying; I just cannot smile like that.

Suddenly, I notice an object in her outstretched hand. I focus on it, hearing the almost imperceptible whirr of my enhanced eyes; closer and closer I bring the object into view.

It is a moth, a large moth, with a wing span of about four inches. Pale green with delicate tracings of brown and darker green, it nestles into her hand. She offers it to the person behind the camera.

I close my eyes and feel the moth tickling my hand. A smile of wonder and love crosses my mouth, her smile. And I hear my voice.

"Look, my love. Isn't it beautiful? What kind is it, do you know?"

I want to open my eyes and see him approach. But I know that if I do I will find myself back in my room. I do not want to be back in my room; I want to stay here. Here, behind my closed eyes, here, inside the mind of a dead woman, I am finally alive.

So I keep my eyes tightly shut. Even without seeing him I know he is close. An excited blush crawls over my skin; oh, yes, he is very close.

His hand, much larger than mine and rougher, cups the bottom of my hand. "It's a luna moth," he says. "Strange that it's out and flying so early in the year. And yes, it is beautiful, but not as much as you."

He takes me into his arms and the moth is forgotten. In her mind.

In my mind I know that he has crushed and killed the creature in his rush to possess her, to possess me. I know who he is. And I hate him. As much as she loves him.

Maybe even more.

"Jenny?"

I jump and turn away from the wall; he stands in the doorway of my room. Drawn to me by the memory? I stare at him with eyes the same color as the moth's wings and wonder. Why is he here? Why am I?

"Have you finished reading?" he asks. "That was quick, even for you."

I don't answer. I can't answer. I'm unable to say the words I want to say.

But I can think them. You killed it, you bastard. It was beautiful, so beautiful. She loved it, I loved it and you killed it.

"Good," he says, taking my silence as assent. He moves further into the room and I back away from him, fearing him, yet remembering the warmth from his closeness and the brush of the dead moth's wings. His eyes stare into mine and I see a flicker of emotion in them. But what emotion? I am too unskilled at such matters to know. Then his eyes move away to the photos on the wall and change to a cold dark gray before he turns his back and walks out of the room.

"Jenny?" He pauses in the hallway.

"Yes?"

"Put your clothes back on."

"I think it's time for you to go out in public." The next morning is come and we breakfast together. Neither of us makes mention of the previous night.

"But won't people recognize me?"

"Perhaps. At the very least, they'll think you look familiar. But the public is fickle with a short memory span." He falls silent for a second. "Yes, it is time," he says, his voice lower now, "time for you to do what you were made to do."

And what was I made to do? The unspoken question lies before us, a challenge and a plea, unanswered.

So he dresses me up in a dead woman's clothes and takes me out. Night after night he shows me off to his acquaintances, his colleagues and the world in general. I grow used to the stares and the whispers. I grow accustomed to the crowds and the conversations. I laugh at the jokes, my comments are witty and my appreciation of the arts and music what they should be. I fit into his world.

I do it well and he is pleased. I can tell by the glow in his eyes when I pass by him this night, on my way to the bathroom. The visit is a pretense, of course, since I have no natural functions. But the woman I was would have gone and so must I.

The room is empty when I get there so I need not pretend. Instead I stand in front of the mirror for a time, staring at my face, wondering where she is. The woman with the moth, with the smile of love lighting her face, where did she go? What happened that she should be dead and I was made to take her place?

With one hand I reach out and touch the cold smooth surface of a reflected cheek. With the other I touch my own face, also cold and smooth. I close my eyes and cannot tell the difference, until one hand becomes wet. I've been crying. For her? I wonder. Or for him? And then, oh, what sorrow have I opened onto?

"Don't ever do that to me again." He stands behind me.

"What?" I stammer, unable to understand his anger, trying to find an answer, a reason.

"Don't try to justify yourself. This isn't a game, it isn't a script someone else has written for you. Real lives are left on the stage when you make your exit."

"My love," I start to speak, but he puts a strong hand over my mouth.

"I am not your love," he growls the words, "you have proved that over and over. Damnable tramp, sniffing around when you get restless, then turning tail and running before it all gets too real."

He turns me around and grips my shoulders, frowning at my tear-filled eyes. "Don't you dare cry." His mouth comes down hard on mine; not a show of love, but of anger. Hurting and bruising though it is, I lean into it, open myself to it and to him.

"No!" Helpless before the wave of memory which washes over me, I gasp at the coldness of his words, the cruelty. Even more startling is her total response of submission and love. She understands and accepts. I can't.

I don't want to remember this; it hurts too much. I open my eyes, but the memory remains. Oh, I think, this is how love feels. I know that she loves him. I can feel the responses deep within me. But the creature that I am does not love, cannot love. I force myself to remember the moth instead, crushed to the desert floor, telling myself that I cry for it and for her. Not for him. Never for him.

"I wish to go home." I have made my way back through the crowded restaurant and come to stand behind his chair. My voice, although soft, carries over the conversation of the table. The other men sitting there stare at me then back at him.

"But, Jenny, my dear," he slides around slowly in his chair, his movement subtly threatening, snake like, "I do not wish to go home. We will stay for a while."

"No." I taste the word in my mouth and find that I like it. So I toss my head back and say it again. "No.

You may stay as long as you like. I will go home."

He looks at me as if he might crush me. He stands slowly and I shrink back into myself. Deep inside my mind I hear a voice, her voice. Do not make him angry, not in public, not in front of others. "No," I say again, ignoring the voice, ignoring the fear, "I do not wish to stay. I am going home."

His fists clench; his eyes bore deep into mine, steelgrey and cold. Then, unexpectedly, they soften and he laughs.

"See, gentlemen," he says to the table of expectant faces, "so much like the original woman. Headstrong and independent. Have you ever seen such perfection in an artificial being?"

The men shake their heads and laugh, but the women seem nervous about his bluntness. As, perhaps, they should be. It could just as easily have been one of them he'd replaced. Some of them, I am sure, have been the objects of his dubious affections. I can tell by the bruised look in their eyes when they meet his.

"Very well, Jenny," he says, his voice sounds amused and patronizing, "we will go home."

His good humor lasts exactly as long as it takes to engage a taxi. He slides his card in the slot and gives the driver our destination, then turns to me, his eyes dark and angry.

"Don't ever do that to me again."

I remember the words. I feel them deep inside me, the sadness they bring with them leaves a bitter, metallic taste in my mouth. Tears fill my eyes and I turn my head away.

He reaches over and grabs my chin. "Are you crying?" He touches the tears on my face; I flinch away from his hand and he laughs. "Yes, you are crying. This is wonderful, Jenny. Absolutely wonderful. A real breakthrough."

"You never thought it wonderful when she cried," I say to him, turning away again. "You forbade her to

do it."

"How can you know that?"

I don't answer him. He takes me by the shoulders and shakes me. "How the hell can you know that?"

I just look at him and smile. And when the cab pulls up to the house, I get out without a word. I go to my room and lock the door.

Cruelty is easier to learn than love.


Morning again and now he is being charming. I enter the dining room and he stands and smiles, pulls out my chair so that I can sit. I see that he has left a single daisy lying by my breakfast plate.

"You are remembering, Jenny," he says as I sip the hot nutro-drink from my mug. "That is why you were crying last night. But you shouldn't cry about it. I want you to remember who you are."

"Who I was, you mean."

"No, who you are. You are Jenny. You have always been Jenny. And you always will be."

"Why?"

He doesn't answer the question. "This is happening sooner than it ever has before."

"What is happening? What do you mean?"

His eyes shift away from mine. "In my previous research, the others only became aware of who they were quite late in the process."

"Others?" Although I know that there must have been others, this startles me. "There have been others?"

He laughs. "So like a real woman. No, there were none like you, Jenny. But yes, there have been others."

"What happened to them?"

"They failed."

"What happened to her? Did she fail, too?"

A twinge of pain passes over his face. "In a way, I suppose she did. She died. But let us not talk of death. I have a surprise for you." He reaches into his pocket and produces two small magnetic cards. "Tickets to Mexico," he says, picking up my hand and kissing it softly. "Now that you have become a woman, I must start treating you as one. It's like a new start for us."

I don't want to go to Mexico. I don't want him kissing my hand. And yet, as he smiles at me over the table, something within responds to him, remembers him and sighs.

I know this place. Not just from the picture hanging on the wall in my room. I know it. As I know the hotel room into which we were admitted. As I know the strength of his arms about me and the touch of his lips on mine. As I know the love she felt for him.

Only when I am alone does it happen that I do not love him. Without his charismatic presence I can remember that he is cruel and thoughtless, arrogant and selfish. I remember his temper, his forcefulness; he frightens and confuses me. But then he does not leave me alone much. We are always together. Often, though, as he sleeps next to me, I think of the others. Not as often as I think of her, but they are there, along with her, shadowy figures in the back of my mind. They whisper to me of his anger and the high cost of their failures. "We did not fail ourselves," they say, "we failed him and that is the same."

And so we come to the desert. To take pictures, he says. A moonlit picnic, he says. A moment of perfection in an imperfect world.

This has all been done before, I remember with a shock. I have worn this dress for him, danced barefoot in the sand for him. And I know now this is why I have been created. For him to have this moment one more time. He is smiling and laughing and relaxed. And I am happy. I love him. I know that my smile is now her smile.

And yet, it is wrong. I turn to him, where he lies on the blanket, his eyes half-shut, his naked skin glowing in the moonlight. "Richard," I say, unable to stop the words, hearing the echoes of other voices saying the words in unison, "we cannot go on like this. There must be an end."

He pushes up on one elbow and stares at me. "What did you say?"

"I want to go home."

He laughs. "You have no home, other than with me, Jenny. No other purpose in life. I thought you knew that."

I close my eyes and the memories pour through me, moving my lips, controlling my words. "I have a home. I have children. You do not wish to share in this home. You want me as a trophy, not as a woman. And as much as I love you, I can't stay. This is wrong."

I feel a slap across my face and open my eyes.

"Jenny," he says, "this is not you speaking. You must stop remembering now. Do not fail me in this."

"I can't stop remembering." I begin to cry. "And it is me speaking. I am your Jenny. I am her. And I can't stay. You know this is true."

He sighs, gets up from the blanket and begins to put on his clothes. "Yes, it is true. Now close your eyes, Jenny, and remember what always happens next."

Conditioned to obey, I close my eyes. And remember his large hands fastening around my neck, crushing and bruising. I do not just remember. He is choking me now and I am gasping for breath. "You won't leave me," he says, "you can't leave me." I hear many versions of his voice saying the same words, over and over. "I'll see you dead and buried first." His grip tightens and he lifts me up off my feet. I kick against him feebly, but my limbs grow limp in remembered response. He drops me to the desert sand then and falls to his knees next to me, crying.

"You were right," he says, "this is wrong. I never want you to die. I keep hoping it will be different. Each new time I keep hoping that you won't remember. Not this. I never wanted you to remember this. And now you have failed me. The best of them all. And I have to start over again. I can't help myself. I have to start it all over again." He packs up the picnic stuff now, putting it all back into its basket. Soon he will leave and I will be alone.

I know that I am to lie still now and let the sand blow over me as the others had before me. After all, I am dead. I remember being dead and I know why I am dead. He has crushed me as he did the moth, as he did her, as he did all the others. They loved him and I loved him. But he has left me alone and I do not love him when I am alone.

I feel a small tickling in the palm of my outstretched hand. I should not feel anything, I am dead. I look over with eyes that should not see and focus on a moth. A beautiful creature, with wings such a delicate green, etched in brown. I smile. And silently I stand, rising to my feet, still cradling the moth. Then I twitch my hand, letting it fly free into the night sky. Knowing as I do so that if the moth lives, so could I and so could she. And I know what I must do, what I was created to do.

"There must be an end," I say as I walk toward him and my hands grip his throat. "And that end is yours."

No one will cry at his funeral. There will be no vids of the event, no mention of his passing. No one will know that he is dead. And no one, but the moth, and the Mexican moon will know that I, of all of them, did not fail him.

Perhaps I loved him more than I knew.

*See also Forever.*

## ONE GREEN CANDLE

Susan Black looked around her uneasily. It wouldn't do to have any of her church friends find her here — outside the small occult bookstore that she'd helped to picket on occasion. But the street was happily deserted and she breathed a sigh of relief. She struggled to open the door, not an easy task burdened as she was, attempting to keep a firm grip on Joshua and James, while maneuvering the stroller occupied by six-month old Mary and balancing purse and diaper bag on her slender shoulder.

The bell on the door rang with a curiously discordant sound that made Susan jump in guilt. She wished now that she hadn't come at all, but her decision had been made, right or wrong. It was her only choice. After all, she thought, I'm fighting for my life and for my children's future.

"May I help you?" The woman behind the counter certainly didn't look like one of the spawn of Satan. Her eyes were a warm, watery blue beneath the thick lenses of her glasses and her smile seemed motherly, welcoming.

"Well," Susan began uncertainly, "I'd like a book of, er, well, spells." She whispered the last word, all too aware of the listening ears of Joshua and James. Once again she doubted her wisdom in being here, wondering if news of her visit would somehow filter back to Pastor Higgins. But the boys' attention was fully occupied by the display case of jewelry; three-year old James was pressing his face up against the glass; Joshua, one whole year older and wiser, was examining the necklaces.

"Look at all the stars, Mummy," he exclaimed, "lots and lots of stars and moons. I can count them all."

"That's nice, dear," Susan said absently and turned her attention back to the woman at the counter.

"Spells, is it?" The clerk gave her a stern, discerning glance over the top of her glasses. "Anything in particular?"

"Well, I don't really know..." Susan's voice trailed off, then rose loudly, "James, quit licking that glass." She turned back to the woman, "I'm sorry, I, I guess I should have left them at home. But I couldn't get a babysitter and my husband, well, he's gone."

The dull finality of that last word caused tears to spring into Susan's eyes, but she wiped them away angrily. "Not dead, you understand," she continued, "just gone. Took off with another woman and left me, with the kids and the house and the bills."

"Honey, I can see you have your hands full. But I don't quite understand why you've come here. Wouldn't your church and minister be a better place to lay your problems?"

"My church?"

"I remember you; I never forget a face. You were here about a month ago, carrying a sign, reading, I believe," and the woman smiled, to Susan's surprise, "'The spawn of Satan shop here.'"A deep blush of embarrassment covered Susan's cheeks. "Actually, I don't much mind, honey, all that publicity brought in business like crazy. Sort of wish, now that things are quiet again, that your group would come back. But a good churchgoing girl like yourself shouldn't be seeking help from an old lady like me. Go back and talk to your minister; he should be able to help you."

"I did." Susan's voice rose in anger. "He told me to accept my lot in life, sell my house, get a job, and put my kids into church-sponsored day care where they can get proper raising. He told me that if I had been the kind of wife that John had needed, he wouldn't have left me. He said if I had done my wifely duty more often, John wouldn't have strayed."

"Wifely duty?" The clerk smiled briefly. "That's how he put it, your wifely duty?"

"Yeah, and it was a duty, too. I never liked it, never wanted to . . ." Susan blushed again, "But I gave him three beautiful children. Isn't that enough? Did I have to enjoy it, too?"

The woman gave a nod, "Some men are like that, honey. What you really need is another man."

"Oh, no," Susan said, "I don't want another man. I just want John back. Pastor says that it's a woman's job to submit to the wishes of her husband, and that her wishes and wants don't matter, that my refusals were sinful in the eyes of God and Jesus."

"Ah, men," the other woman said scornfully, "Men. I see. Oh, Goddess, how I see." Susan felt the clerk's sudden rush of sympathy for her as she came out from behind the counter and walked over to the book shelves, pulling out a large volume. "These are white spells, for the most part, not much harmful in here."

"But will they help?"

"Well, now, that depends on you, honey. First you must believe, then you must desire. And it's not like a cookbook, you know, not everyone can use these 'recipes.'"

"Have you used them?"

The woman laughed. "It's been a long time since I ever desired anything badly enough to want to try. But I have and they have worked. And I've also discovered that sometimes getting what we think we want can backfire. We all carry wishes within us that should not be fulfilled." She held the book out to Susan.

Susan hesitated then accepted the book, clasping it against her chest, "But I know what I want, that's easy. I want John back home with us again, forever. How could wishing for that be bad. And how could that ever backfire?"

"Even so," the woman said, walking back behind the counter and ringing up the sale. "Even so."

The book sat on the top shelf of the bedroom closet for days. Every time Susan opened the door she saw it, felt it, waiting there to seduce her with its dubious wisdom. She didn't care that the woman had said that the spells were white and not harmful, Susan knew deep in her heart that it was bad. That God and Jesus would not approve.

And most especially, Pastor Higgins would not approve. He paid a visit to her home the following Sunday afternoon. Susan had always dreaded his unexpected arrivals, knowing that the time he chose would always be the worst possible one. That day was no exception, James and Joshua were cranky and recalcitrant, having refused their afternoon naps and Mary was cutting a new tooth. The living room floor was strewn with toys, the dining room table was covered with papers and bills that Susan had been attempting to understand. She'd just barely managed to dress herself in faded sweatshirt and jeans when the doorbell rang.

"Susan," Pastor Higgins nodded, almost smiling, as she opened the door. "We missed you at church this morning. I hope nothing is wrong."

Flustered, Susan ushered him into the living room, sweeping the couch clear of tiny cars and plastic superheroes. "Yes, I know, I'm sorry, we overslept, and Mary's been fussy all day."

"The Lord accepts no alibis, Susan, and no substitutes."

"Yes, well, can I offer you something, a cup of tea, maybe, or coffee?"

Susan was not disappointed when he refused. "No, thank you, I can't stay too long." He brushed at the crumbs on his trouser leg that he'd picked up from the sofa cushion. "I wanted to tell you that John and that woman attended services this morning. I must say that she seemed quite charming, not what I had expected at all. I even had brunch at their home, such a charming and clean environment. It would be so good for the children."

"So what's your point?" Susan was startled as the words she normally only thought burst aloud from her lips.

"Only that John asked for my help in obtaining custody of the children, a character reference sort of thing, and I agreed. You see, it is my duty in the eyes of God to make sure that your children receive the correct upbringing, a Christian upbringing, and quite honestly, Susan," his eyes raked over the room, taking in the dust and the mess, "I don't see them getting it here."

As if to punctuate his reasoning, James and Joshua ran into the room, naked and screaming. "Mummy," James wailed, "Joshua says my wee-wee is getting smaller and smaller and smaller and soon it'll just fall off and I'm gonna turn into a girl, just like Mary. I don't wanna be a girl."

Joshua wiggled his bare hips, "Girlie, girlie, James is gonna be a girlie!"

James ran over and butted Joshua in the chest with his head and they both tumbled onto the floor, a tangle of naked arms, legs and flailing fists. "I don't wanna be a girl, I don't wanna be a girl."

Pastor Higgins' eyebrows rose as he got up from the couch and headed to the door, "No discipline," he muttered, "no guidance."

"They're only kids, Pastor Higgins," Susan hated the pleading note that entered her voice, "this is the way kids are. They play, they fight, they get dirty and they make a mess. But they need me, need to stay with me, I'm their mother."

"By birth only, Susan, and sometimes the Lord has a different plan to take care of his little lambs. I hope to see you in church soon."

She waved to him from the screen door and watched his car pull out of the driveway and down the street. Then she slammed the door. "See me in church soon?" she whispered, "not on your frigging life," and burst into tears.

"Mummy," Joshua came up to her and hugged his naked body to her leg, "don't cry. Daddy will come home soon, and everything will be better. You can make it better, Mummy, I know you can. You make everything better."

Susan reached down and rumpled his hair, "I will make it better, Josh, I promise. You go get your clothes on, right now, young man. And you too, James."

"But, Mummy, what if my wee-wee falls off while I have my undies on? I'd never know it."

She looked down at his worried face. "Your wee-wee won't fall off, James. I promise. And you know I always keep my promises."

"Yay!" both boys yelled in unison, scampering back to their room, their disagreement completely forgotten.

Later that night, Susan removed the book of spells from the closet shelf. Her hands shook, but she was resolved that this book was her last resort. Pastor Higgins made it very apparent that he would not help her in her struggle, in fact, he had betrayed her trust and gone over to the other side, John's side. And now they were all plotting to take away her children: John, Pastor, even Jesus. Susan knew she would do anything to prevent that from happening. She loved her children, didn't want them raised by another woman; she wanted the best for them, a home with mother and father there together. A devoted father, who would never leave her or the children for another woman.

"Men," she muttered as she paged through the book, mimicking the old woman in the book store, "they don't think with their brains, that's for sure. They allow themselves to be led about by something else." She smiled to herself, thinking about the fight the boys'd had that afternoon, thinking how it might be a good thing if all men had happen to them what Joshua had teased James about. Without that, John would have stayed here where he belonged.

Susan continued flipping the pages of the book, browsing through the spells as through a catalog. She stopped and read over a few, curious as to how they were said, how they were accomplished. Finally she found a set of love spells, four pages worth. The first two were for new love, the second were for the return of an old love. Some had long lists of ingredients, things that she knew she'd have to spend a long time finding. But one caught her eye. It was easy, it was simple and better than anything, it seemed less demonic than some of the others, requiring only the burning of one green candle for seven days and a fervent wish of the heart.

She opened a drawer in the buffet and pulled out an evergreen-scented candle left over from Christmas. "Here goes nothing," she giggled and lit the candle. Turning out all the other lights in the house, she composed her thoughts, working out her wish. "John," she whispered over the open flame, making it flicker and dance, "I want John back, pure and untouched by temptations of the flesh."

The week of burning the candle went quickly, by the seventh night there was only a stub left. Susan pronounced her wish one last time, the same one she had said every night since that first one. The candle flame flared up quickly, hurting her eyes; she jumped back just in time to avoid being burned. And as the candle sputtered and went out, leaving only a small puddle of wax on the holder, the phone rang.

"Hello." She tried to make her voice as nice as possible, knowing that it was John calling.

"Mrs. Black?" a detached female voice questioned,

"Mrs. John Black?"

"Yes?"

"This is General City Hospital. We've just admitted your husband and he asked us to call. He's been injured, I'm afraid, not life-threatening, but you should probably come to see him as soon as you can."

"I'll be right there."


"How are the kids?" John stared up at Susan, his face white and strained. She patted his hand, then reached over and stroked his cheek.

"They're fine, John. I called Cindy to come over and watch them while I left. They were sleeping, I doubt that they'll even know I'm gone."

"I've missed them."

Susan nodded, "And?"

"I've missed you, too, honey. I don't know what I was thinking to leave you. You're the best wife a man could ever have."

"What about her?"

"After what she did to me, how could I ever forgive her, ever love her? I'll never love another woman but you. I realized that before, um, well, before." His eyes darted around the room and a grimace of pain and embarrassment crossed his face. "And when I told her that, when I got ready to leave tonight, she went crazy, went into the knife drawer," tears began to fall from his eyes, "she cut me, she hurt me bad, Susan...

"I know, John, I know."

"But I'm not a full man now, Susan, you know, and I can never..."

"It's okay, John," Susan said softly, hiding her triumphant smile. "You're back now, and that's all that matters."

*Mike Resnick asked me to do a story for DAW's Return of the Dinosaurs and I ended up writing this. I was thrilled when he accepted it, figuring that perhaps this sweet little tale of an intergalactic cosmetic saleswoman and the pterodactyl who loved her was probably not quite what he was expecting. This story also has the dubious distinction of being the only thing I've ever written involving skinny-dipping and hang gliders. Published on its own for Amazon Kindle recently, it spent some time at the #2 slot of Dinosaur Romances.*

## ROMEO FALLING

"Goddamned piece of space junk!" I stopped my foot an easy inch away from delivering a sharp kick to the control panel. Yeah, the stupid ship was already down, but it was probably fixable; damaging it further wouldn't do me any good, despite how wonderful it would have felt.

"Good plan, girlfriend. Knock out all your controls while you are at it." The tones of the computer's speech module were sarcastic and comfortingly familiar, as they were designed to be, since they were my own voice patterns repeated back to me. I'd tried all the available voices and they'd all annoyed me. What I'd finally ended up with was very similar to carrying on a prolonged conversation with myself. But space was a big lonely place and I was all I had.

"No harm done. I stopped."

"Just barely. Now, do you want to know what your options are?"

"Yeah, let me have it."

As things turned out, I wasn't in too much trouble. I'd managed to land with minimal damage when the warnings had gone off. I'd also managed to land on an oxygen-based planet, with acceptable food and water rations, should I be down for longer than my meager supplies lasted. That, however, was the extent of the good news. The planet was listed as non-humanoid/ non-intelligent/non-populated and the necessary parts for repair to my ship would take at least one or two months to arrive via auto-shuttle. In addition, I'd definitely miss my cosmetics drop off at Megalon IV. By the time I would finally arrive, the tints would be all wrong, passé, last week's news. Worse, I was certain that the other company's ships would have already been there and gone. Those damned pink monstrosities, just the look of them made me nauseous; they should, in my opinion, be banned from space.

In addition, none of this took into account the fact that this run was supposed to give me the down payment on a new ship. Now the missed drop and the repairs would set me back even further. I often wondered why I did this. There were times when I just wanted to give up on the whole thing, settle down somewhere, anywhere, and make a life. To be honest, any life would be better than the one I had.

"Shit."

"Oh, and by the way, that reminds me," the computer voice droned on, smugly. Damn, I could be an insufferable bitch at times. "Your little emergency landing was a bit difficult on the sanitary facilities. I've ordered an extra pump and a valve or two along with the other necessities, but for now, you'd better go al-fresco."

"Great. Just great." Now that we'd mentioned it, I realized that nature was indeed calling. "So," I said, getting up from my chair and slinging a holstered stunner over my shoulder, "Anything special I should be careful of out there?"

"No. There is nothing much out of the ordinary."

"Good."

"Unless, of course, you count the dinosaurs."

My legs gave way underneath me and I thumped back into the seat. "The what?"

"Di-no-sau-ers," it said in my best derogatory fashion, "Prehistoric earth creatures, dating back some 150 million years. The term itself comes from two ancient Greek words . . ."

"Yeah, yeah, I know what dinosaurs are." I sighed, seriously considering re-configuring the voice module, convenient though it was for singing self-harmony. "But what the hell are they doing here?"

"This place is coded as a non-operational recreational planet."

"Any information about why it's now non-operational?"

There was a slight pause. "Overall incompatibility of the genetically-designed life forms with the visiting life forms. It has been closed down for about a hundred years. Supposedly non-dangerous, though, so you should be perfectly safe."

I nodded slowly. "Thank you. Supposedly. Should be. I feel so much better." Standing up, I took a deep breath and headed for the exit. "'Join the Merchant's League,'" I mimicked the vid-ad, "'grow rich beyond your wildest dreams, and see the wonders of the universe.'" The computer gave a noise that could have been a snort. I agreed. Well, I thought, as I switched open the door, maybe the wonders part will be accurate.

The planet, or at least the part on which we'd landed, was breathtakingly beautiful; it had a sparse, almost Earth "Old West" appearance: sandy, rocky and flat with what looked like a small mountain range on the horizon. I knew that appearances were deceiving in this kind of terrain, those mountains could be immensely high. The air had a clear crystal scent and feel. Scrub brush grew in a scattered fashion, but a splash of not too distant green promised a watering hole.

Deciding to save that trip for a little later, and with my hand firmly fixed on my stunner, I glanced around uneasily, but saw nothing more than a few small, purple, six-legged lizards, obviously indigenous creatures, possibly a food source for the purported dinosaurs.

"Well," I said, "First things first." My voice sounded muffled, swallowed up in the vastness of the area, but was still loud enough to cause the lizards to skitter away for shelter. I spotted an appropriate clump of small bushes, squatted down among them and relieved myself, then laughed as I fastened up my suit. Why on earth was I seeking privacy? There was no one here to watch.

*Pardon me, I couldn't help but notice that you just thought about earth.*

The voice was masculine, deep, drawling and seemed to originate directly inside my mind. I spun around. "Jesus!" Lounging rather indolently against the side of my ship stood a six foot tall, bright red, leather-winged, lizard-headed bird.

*Romeo, actually. And you won't need that.*

"What?" My hand had been edging slowly toward my stunner.

*My name. You obviously have mistaken me for someone else. My name is Romeo. I sense your fear, but assure you that you don't need your weapon. And since I mean you no harm, I will trouble you no longer.*

With a sweep of his wings he was gone, diminishing first to a small vee shape, then to a speck in the sky, and then to nothing at all. My knees were shaking. I was thankful, as I quickly entered the ship and switched the exit closed and locked, that I'd relieved myself before the confrontation.

"Nicely handled," the computer commented on my return.

"Shut up. It scared me, is all. I was hardly expecting something like that, waiting for me. And it spoke, telepathically or something. Weird."

"I did warn you."

"Well, yeah, you did. Just barely. Get out all the files you can find about this planet and let's have a look at exactly what kind of god-forsaken place we're stranded on, shall we?"

I spent the next two days reviewing all that information known about this planet. Unfortunately, there wasn't that much. And what was there was old news. I watched some of the early vid-ads importuning rich space travelers to "Come and Partake of the Wonders of Prehistory." Not much of a slogan, I thought scornfully, but then the whole planet was a project left entirely in the hands of the scientists who'd thought it up. Always a bad marketing idea. When things didn't quite work out the way they'd planned, they just closed it down. Idiots. They must've lost millions.

And their dinosaurs weren't really dinosaurs. They were genetic constructs of what these particular scientists thought dinosaurs should be. All of the creatures were artificially created, with the data from original DNA samples collected and consulted, but not always used. The occupants of this planet were mongrels, put together from a piece of this and a piece of that, not pure and not simple, with incredibly long life spans. Each species was encoded with a special, often stereotypical personality to make them more amenable to the artificial situation. And in some cases, this personality type was ominously slanted to prevent certain types of instinctual behavior. Mostly, the system was designed to prevent wanton and possibly destructive over-procreation. The tyrannosaurs and some of the other carnivores, for example, were almost exclusively homosexual in orientation. The larger plant eaters were reclusive loners and the smaller ones were equipped with a messianic complex. This, of course, explained Romeo's recognition of the name I had invoked. In fact, all of these artificial personalities made sense to me from that perspective. It would take two members of the species to act out of type to enable a successful mating, thus maintaining the ecological balance desired.

"Except the personality for the winged dinosaurs," I concluded in discussing the situation with the computer, "they are listed as the hopelessly romantic type. How on earth does that prevent procreation? I'd think it would mean they'd breed like rabbits."

"The files don't contain that information."

"Yeah, I noticed." I got up from the console and sighed. "Well, whatever these creatures may be, there's absolutely no indication that they present a threat to human-kind. In fact, they seem to have been purposely designed to be totally benevolent to two-legged types."

"All available data would indicate that, yes. I concur."

I stretched my arms up over my head, sniffed, then groaned. "As for me, I think I'm way overdue for a bit of a bath. I've gotten a little ripe, cooped up in this tin can with no use of sanitary facilities except for a few bushes. And since my winged Romeo seems to have disappeared, I think I'll hit the watering hole."

"Take the stunner."

I shrugged. "Why? If anything on this planet wanted me, they'd have come for me already. They've had opportunities in my many potty trips. I can't hide inside forever, cowering in fear. So I'll just take a couple of towels and a bar of soap, if you don't mind."

"Suit yourself. But if something else happens, don't say I didn't warn you adequately."

I stuck my tongue out at the console on the way to the supplies cabinet. Did I usually sound that much of a know-it-all? As I walked out the door, towels slung over my shoulder, a cake of soap, and a water-testing kit stashed in my pocket, I made a mental note to have the entire computer system re-worked when I finally got off this planet.

Outside it was another beautiful day: sunny and hot, but not terribly oppressive thanks to the slight breeze blowing in from the mountains. Stiff and sore from two solid days of sitting at the ship's controls, I decided to jog over to where I'd spotted the waterhole. Yes, there it was, larger than I'd expected -- more like a small, but deep lake. The water was clear, I could see all the way to the bottom and nothing swam in this lake but more of the six-legged lizards I'd encountered before. I scanned the area for the skeletons of dead animals or any other indication that the water might be poisonous. To my relief, nothing at all indicated a problem. But to be safe, I put a small drop of water into the testing-kit tube and sat it and me on a nearby flat rock, to wait for the results. The sun was hot and a blinding glare came off the water. I unzipped my suit and stepped out of it, took off my undergarments and tossed them all into the water for a nice long soak. Then I stretched out on the sun-warmed rock, wiggled my toes, and closed my eyes, humming a song to myself.

I must've fallen asleep almost immediately, a combination of the heat and the peacefulness of the pond. I dreamed: a long, winding dream involving the high cliffs of the faraway mountain range and the sensation of soaring and gliding over the desert floor far beneath me. A voice sang to me in my dream, a beautiful song, and a beautiful voice. Masculine, deep, and slow-pitched, it warmed my soul as the sun warmed my body, wrapping me in love and leather wings.

*Excuse me,* the voice sang, *I do not wish to disturb your rest, but I saw you here and knew that we must speak.*

No, I thought as I struggled to open my eyes, that voice is not part of the dream. I remember that voice.

"Romeo?"

*You remembered me. How wonderful.*

I squinted up at him where he loomed over me, still confused with the heat and the dream.

*You are not afraid of me now. That is good.*

I realized when I sat up that he was right. I wasn't afraid of him, although I knew that I should be. This was a ferocious prehistoric creature, capable of shredding me to pieces with vicious claws. It didn't matter that I knew his kind had been created artificially, to be benevolent toward humanoids. It had been a hundred years since anything but dinosaurs had walked this planet; they could have developed some nasty instincts since then.

You should have brought the stunner, my mind said, or you should turn and run for the ship. But I wasn't afraid. I felt secure and totally relaxed as I sat naked on the rock and smiled up at this creature. He even seemed to smile back, though I knew that wasn't possible.

*You merely sense my happiness at meeting you again. I do not actually have the facial muscles necessary to smile. You, on the other hand, have a beautiful smile. You have such nice, white, even teeth. And your skin is such a glorious shade of red.*

"Red?" I looked down at my naked body. He was right. My skin was almost the same shade of red as his. "Damn, I must've slept longer than I'd thought. This isn't my skin's natural color, you know, it's sunburn."

*It is still a beautiful color, don't you think?*

I stared at him, then laughed, delighted and somehow not at all surprised that the masculine ego knew no barrier of species. "Yeah, I suppose it is.

He reached a wing over and covered my arm. *We are a perfect match.*

I shivered slightly at his touch and his words. The feeling of love from the dream washed back over me and I blushed an even deeper red. What did this creature want from me? Why was I even talking to him? I didn't need friends, didn't have time for them; didn't stay long enough in one place to keep them. And I liked my solitude.

But something deep within my mind denied that statement: the same thing that had warmed to his presence and his touch, held no fear of his alienness. Personal contact was something I hadn't had in a very long time and I liked it. Maybe too much.

"Well, it's been nice talking to you," I said, avoiding his intent eyes, "but I came out here for a much needed bath. So if you'll excuse me..." I stood up, verified the safety of the water in the test tube, and dove into the pool.

Cold. Damn, the water was incredibly cold. I came up to the surface sputtering and he still stood on the rock. I could hear him laugh inside my head.

*I could have warned you about that, you know. But you didn't ask. There are warmer pools around, I can show you if you wish.*

"No," I insisted through clenched teeth, "this is just fine. Now if you don't mind, I'd like a little privacy." He stared at me for a while, nodded.

*Of course, I understand. You wish to bathe alone.*

"Yeah, thanks." I paddled over to where my suit still floated and fumbled around inside the wet material to find my bar of soap. I began to work up a lather in my hands, glanced back up at him, and said with a note of finality, "It was nice to see you again."

Romeo flexed his incredible wings then cocked his reptilian head at me. *Perhaps it is presumptuous of me, but I would like to know your name.*

"Oh, yeah, my name. I'm sorry. I'm Miranda."

*Miranda? Do not be sorry, Miranda. It is a beautiful name for a beautiful woman. Until later, then,* and he bowed slightly. Perhaps he was just preparing for flight, I couldn't tell. *I bid you farewell.*

"Yeah, see you later."

After he had disappeared from sight, I gently soaped my burned skin, washed my clothes, and went back to the ship, singing softly to myself the song from the dream.

"Have a nice bath?" The computer's tone was snide as usual, but I was in too good a mood to rise to the bait.

"Very nice," I said pleasantly. "Do we have any sunburn cream in storage?"

There was a pause as it checked the records. "No. Nothing at all like that."

"Oh, well . . ."

*Excuse me. I do not wish to interrupt.* Romeo stood hesitantly at the door of the ship, clutching a bouquet of blood-red flowers in his right wing claw. *These are for you, Miranda.*

"Flowers?" I blushed again and the computer snorted. "Thanks."

*Crush them and rub the juice on you. I believe they will help soothe your skin where it has been burned by the sun. I would offer to do it for you, but I'm afraid my limbs are not designed for that purpose.*

I smiled and took the flowers from him. "Thanks," I said again, "it's very thoughtful of you."

*You are most welcome.* He gave a gesture that could have been a shrug and flew away.

"Flowers? From an admirer?"

"From a friend. For medicinal purposes."

"Uh-huh. I felt the tension between the two of you. You have an admirer."

I shook my head and gave a nervous laugh. "Give me a break, will you? We're different species."

"Different species, maybe, but we have scientific proof that the creature is a hopeless romantic. I would advise no further contact with him, or with any of the other species on this planet."

That did it. I could put up with the snide comments, the sarcastic tones, but I didn't need a stupid machine making decisions about the company I kept. "Oh, bloody hell, who died and made you my mother? It was interesting, talking with him. But it wasn't anything more than that. It gets kind of lonely, sometimes, all cooped up in this ship with no company, no one intelligent to talk to for months on end."

"I talk to you. I am far more intelligent than you deserve. Why would you need anything else? Much less a freak species of animal," the emphasis on the last word was sneering, "which brings you flowers? I heard you arrange to meet him again. Are you crazy? Did you hit your head when you dove in that pool?"

"No, I didn't hit my head. And you talk too damn much." I walked over to the console and for the first time since I'd been traveling, turned off the voice module, vowing not to turn it back on until I was ready to leave. If then.

It was quiet inside the ship after that. But I didn't really mind. Romeo returned every day. And we talked as I swam and sunned myself. Sometimes I would close my eyes and try to imagine him as a humanoid male. It was easy. Frighteningly easy. And the computer was correct about one thing. He was hopelessly romantic. He would sing for me, quote me poetry. His knowledge of earth classics was surprising and when I questioned him about where he obtained it, he just shrugged. He'd always known it. Apparently, it had been genetically programmed into his kind. Romeo was the perfect companion and I felt my normal reserve open under his kindness, his consideration. I'd never known a human male so eager to please, so thrilled to bring gifts and tokens.

The auto-shuttle had arrived with my parts and departed again. Still I stayed on the planet. Somehow I just couldn't face the thought of repairing the ship. I was enjoying my vacation, the first one I'd had in years. Or so I told myself. The truth was I was beginning to like this place. And it's inhabitant.

One day, after I had my swim and was sunbathing, naked on the rocks as usual, Romeo showed up with a very large bottle tightly clutched in his talons. *We will have a party. I obtained this from a rex I know. I think you'll like it, Miranda.*

"What is it?"

*Tequila. An Earth-type liquor. I thought perhaps it might make you happy.*

I smiled at him. "I know what tequila is. The rexes make this?"

*They are better with their forelegs than my kind. And clever about making things to drink and eat. Strange creatures, they are, but they serve a purpose.*

"I see." I reached up, took the proffered bottle, pulled out its cork, and took a long swallow. It burned all the way down and I choked. Romeo patted me on the back with his wing.

*It is not good?*

"No, it's fine. Very good." I took another swig to prove it. "It's just that I haven't had anything this strong to drink in a long time. Have some?"

He cocked his head at me, his eyes intense as usual, but with a strange undercurrent of something I'd never seen before. *May I drink from the bottle with you?*

"How else could you have some?" I was missing some clue here that I should have gotten. But his pleasure at my wanting to share the tequila with him was obvious. "Please, have some."

He squatted down next to me, his back legs curled up underneath him. I held the bottle to his mouth and he grasped down tightly on the neck, tossed his head back, and took a long drink.

*Now it is your turn again. We must drink it all or the rex will be offended.*

I took another drink and giggled. "I will be very drunk if we have to finish the bottle, Romeo. And I'll be no good for conversation."

*Conversation is fine. But sometimes a shared silence is better.*

We continued to pass the bottle back and forth. Each time he drank, he asked my permission again, and each time when I granted it, his eyes would glow with an eagerness I didn't understand. But after half the bottle was gone, it didn't matter. When three-quarters of it was gone, I began to drift away, falling into a delicious languor. Romeo began to sing to me again, a song I remembered from my dream so many weeks ago. And before I knew it, I was curled up under his wing and singing along with him.

The words were strange to me, with a ritualistic quality. Something about his being the last of his kind. And how he would die for his love. Romantic. Hopelessly romantic.

We continued to pass the bottle and my giggling stopped and as the words of the song began to sink into me. It was so sad, him being the last of his kind, wanting to die for love and all that I began to cry. He licked away my tears with his tongue and I shivered at his touch. So foreign and strange, yet so familiar and tender.

When the bottle was finally empty, he took it and flung it out into the lake. I hiccupped slightly. "It's all gone. Now what do we do?"

*Now is the time. I will teach you to fly.*

"Silly Romeo." I reached up and stroked the skin below his eye socket. "I have no wings. I can't fly. But I wish I could. It would be so lovely to fly with you."

*And so you shall, Miranda, my love. It is our destiny.* He flexed his wings and rose from the ground, grasping me beneath the arms as he rose. We soared over the lake, over the desert. I didn't look down, instead I closed my eyes, and just drifted, losing track of time and distance, losing track of everything but the sound of his song.

Only when I felt him gently set me down did I open my eyes. We were in the midst of the distant mountain range. My ship was almost invisible, just a light glinting off a pebble a long way away and a long way down. It didn't matter. Nothing mattered but Romeo's song. Which had stopped. I sat up, amazingly clearheaded, considering what we had just drunk. "Give my regards to the rexes next time you see them," I said with a smile, "that's wonderful tequila."

*As I said, they have their uses. Come with me and I will show you another.*

We entered into a cave set into one of the cliffs. "You live here?"

*As much as it can be said I live anywhere, I suppose. When one has wings, one needn't stay in any one place for too long. Moreover, when one is alone the concept of home is an unknown. But I need not say it. It is a fact you yourself know quite well.* He gave the odd gesture that served as his shrug, and brushed aside a curtain woven of reeds from a side opening. *Here is what I want you to see.*

Ever the gentleman, he stood back and allowed me to proceed him. Prominently displayed in the center of the room was a wing-type device, very close in design to an earth hang-glider, except that the wings were curved and fluted much like Romeo's wings.

I walked over to it. "May I touch it? It looks very delicate."

*You may do with it what you like. It is yours. And it is stronger than it appears.*

I ran my hands over the leather of the wings. They were red, similar in color and texture to Romeo's skin. Too close to be anything but the real thing, I suspected. "It feels like you."

*As it should. It was my father's.*

I gave him a long glance. His father's, I wondered? As in, it belonged to his father? Or as in, the skin was his father's? I didn't want to ask.

"Does it work?"

*Would you like to try it?*

"Me?" My breath caught just a bit in my throat. Fly? Without a ship under my control? Without any kind of safety features?

*It is easy. I will help you. You do trust me, don't you? You do want to fly with me?*

His voice was so confident, so relaxed that any residual fear I might have felt flowed out of me. I looked at him and smiled. "I'd love to."

*Good.* He walked over to me, and enveloped me in a brief hug. We both shivered in the contact and I felt a surge of excitement spin through my body, as if his touch reactivated the liquor we had drunk. Then we carefully carried the glider out of the cave and onto the cliffs.

"So, what exactly do I do?"

Romeo showed me how to grip the glider, making sure that my wrists were wrapped securely in the thick leather straps. The mechanism was amazingly light and I gave him a doubtful look. "Now, you're sure this will hold me? I don't particularly want to go crashing down to the desert floor."

He looked at me reproachfully. *I will be with you, Miranda. Would I allow you to fall?*

"No. I suppose you wouldn't." We walked over to the edge of the cliff together. "Any last words of advice? Before I go hurtling off into the wild blue yonder?"

Romeo stroked my back with his wing. *Keep your wings high. Fly far and fast. And remember that I will always be with you. Always.*

Then he pushed me from the cliff. I barely had time to register the fact that he had, when my wings captured an updraft and I was flying. The blood was pounding in my veins, my eyes were tearing with the wind, but I was flying.

*Do you like it?* Out of the corner of my eye, I caught a glimpse of Romeo, flying to my right and slightly behind me.

"Oh, yes," I called over the wind, "it's wonderful." I experimented with the tilt of the wings and the shift of my body, discovering the control and the feel of the glider. He stayed with me, encouraging my efforts, congratulating my successes, correcting my mistakes. Soon, I felt at ease in the air, growing more confident with each minute. I laughed into the wind. "Romeo, race me to the ship."

I surged ahead of him, picking up speed. Felt him behind me, striving to catch up with me. Felt an overwhelming wash of emotion come from him and flood into my awareness.

I faltered slightly when I realized at last what this was. A mating flight. All the signs were there, the rituals, the courtship, the words and songs of love and romance, clues that would have been obvious had they come from a humanoid male. Yet I had responded to him, more than I ever had to another human. Hell, I probably even loved him. Turning my head, I laughed as I caught sight of him. If he wanted a mating flight, he'd get it. But, I thought with a wicked smile, I wasn't going to make it easy.

"So go ahead and catch me, Romeo," I called tauntingly. "If you can." I veered sharply away from him, making a complete turn at a dizzying speed. And we played in the air, dancing the dance he wanted, while he sang his song for me. I would slow down and allow him to approach, then would glide away out of his grasp. The song in my mind grew more intense with each encounter, until eventually, it began to take over my will, conquering any sense of self. Then I slowed and flew straight.

Romeo caught me as I knew he would, as I wanted him to. He enveloped me with his wings, grasping me around the chest, working his way deep inside me. And oddly enough, I was inside him. We were one creature, not completely human, not completely dinosaur, but something new, gliding over the desert floor. And for the first time in my life I felt loved. Truly and completely loved.

Then we separated and both drifted to the ground. I untangled my wrists from the glider straps and set it aside, lying myself down on the sand. I was laughing, crying, and pulling in air in great gulps. "That was quite a race," I said when I caught my breath, "but I think it was a tie. We will have to try it again, sometime soon."

*There will not be another time, I'm afraid. I thought you understood.*

"Understood what?"

*That I was the last of my kind. And that I would die for your love.*

"Romeo? But you can't die."

*I can and I will, my love. My kind searches for their one true love and when they find her they love her and only her. Then they must die. It is our way, the way we were made.*

"The way you were made?" My voice rose indignantly. "Goddamned scientists. Messing about with lives and emotions they know nothing about. Playing god. How would they like it if they died after having sex? Bastards."

He gave a high-pitched cry. *Destiny cannot be changed, my love. But I will always be with you.*

And he died. There on the desert floor of that truly god-forsaken planet.

"Damn." I sat down next to his body, took his reptilian head onto my lap, and stroked the skin on his face. "If I had known, I never would have flown with you. I didn't realize that the words of the song were true. Damn it, you stupid creature, you should have told me, warned me."

But I realized that he couldn't have told me and wouldn't have warned me. So I did the only thing I could do, I sang his song back to him, cradling his dead body in my arms, through the long cold night and into the next morning.

*Mornin', mum.*

I came out of my trancelike state and glared at the enormous tyrannosaurus rex standing over me. "Morning." I gently displaced Romeo's head from my lap and stood up. "He's dead."

*Aye, I know. We watched the flight. And a mighty flight it was, too; inspirin', you might say. My partner's painting the picture of Romeo falling right now. And I'm here to help you.*

This creature's high-pitched and nasal voice felt strange in my mind, where Romeo's had been for so long. And seemed so incongruous from a creature of his size and strength.

*Aye, those bastard scientists had one helluva strange sense of humor. No wonder they all picked up and left, must've been hard for 'em to live with the perversions they created. Good riddance, say we.*

"I might say the same thing. You say that you're here to help me. What do I need help with?"

*Why the little 'un, of course.*

"The little one?"

*Romeo's son. He was the last of his kind until you came along. Now there will be another.*

"Romeo has a son?"

The rex giggled slightly and shook his head. *These pteros, they're great with the ladies, great with the trappings and the words of love. But they ain't much on explanations.*

I snorted. "I guess not. And as far as I can tell, neither are you."

*You'll give birth to Romeo's son. Plain 'nuff for you?*

"But, how can that be possible? We are different species, completely different creatures."

The rex waved his small forearms in the air. *Genes, strange combinations of DNA, mixin' of stuff that shouldn't be mixed. I can't say I understand myself. The brontos, now, they're the thinkers. They spend all their time alone trying to figure this kind of stuff out. They could explain it to you, if you wanted. But whatever the reason, it's a fact. You're pregnant with Romeo's son.*

I stared at him in shock for a while. Then I smiled.

A son. Romeo's son. "But how will I survive the birth?"

The rex clicked his tongue. *There're dangers of course, but the brontos can help. We got time to work around it. Unless, you wanna leave. Some do. Some go away and never come back. We don't wanna know what happens to the little 'uns in that case. It's not a nice universe out there, far as I can tell.*

"No, it's cold there and lonely. And there's never been anything out there for me. This is the only home I've ever known. I'll stay."

*Thought you might.* He walked over to Romeo's body, picking it up and slinging it over his shoulder. *I'll take care of this here for you. The little 'un will eventually need a glider. And you might wanna be alone for a while. But when you want company, my partner and me live in a cave over in the mountains. Fly by anytime.*

"Thank you. I will. But I'm not alone, you know. He promised."

The rex gave me a great big toothy grin, a wave, and shambled across the desert ground. I watched him for a while, then turned and headed back to my ship, to gather what little I thought I'd need for my new life. And as I went, I sang a song of love, bigger than species, bigger than life. I would want to teach the words to my son.

Deep inside I felt a spark and a tiny voice spoke in my mind. *Heathcliff. My name is Heathcliff.*

I smiled. No, I would never be alone.

*This story was published in a charity anthology, Small Bites, a collection of flash fiction. I've always loved crows and this story may show why.*

## THE TIPS OF HER WINGS

Carolee's breath fogged the cold window as she watched the flock of crows in her front yard. She never grew tired of seeing them, never saw the glint of sunlight on their wings without envying them their freedom, their beauty. "I want to fly," she whispered, smiling as the nearest bird cocked its head. "I want to fly."

She failed to hear his car pull into the driveway. The crows heard it, though, rising to higher ground in a thick cloud of feathers and noise. Carolee sighed and pulled the curtains shut, but not quickly enough to avoid her father's anger.

"What the hell're you looking at? They're rats with wings. Dirty creatures, I should shoot 'em all." He slammed the door, giving the house a cursory glance. Carolee bit her lip. Since the death of her mother she'd been juggling not only her schoolwork but also the household chores. She now knew why her mother had been so meticulous; scrubbing was easier than enduring her father's rants.

He stumbled into the dining room, grunting as he sat down to read the mail she'd left neatly stacked for him. Drunk again, she thought and walked past him into the kitchen to serve dinner.

They ate in silence as always. Carolee stood up when he'd finished and began to clear the table. A sharp pain hit her, followed by a warmth between her legs. She gasped and dropped the plate she carried, only to be rewarded by a slap.

"Clumsy shit. What the hell's wrong with you?"

She knew what was wrong. Her friends at school had already undergone this transformation, and her mother had explained the facts of life to her years ago. But she wasn't prepared for the pain or the utter desolation of feeling so alone.

"I've started," she said quietly, picking up the broken plate.

"Started what?" He swayed on his feet, hand still raised from the last slap.

"My period."

He let out a disgusted breath. "Great. That's exactly what I need right now."

She started to clean the spilled food when he grabbed her arm. "Let's get to the drugstore – don't need blood all over the goddamned house."

The icy road would have made a sober man drive slower. The car went into a spin and hit a tree; Carolee saw it in slow motion, wondering if this was how her mother had died. Had the crows gathered then, as they did now, to escort her from this life?

When her eyes opened the world seemed larger. Her father looked gigantic, thrown through the windshield, sprawled over the hood of the car. The crows covering him, though, were exactly the right size. Carolee's size. Carolee felt an indescribable joy, a thrill from the top of her head to the tips of her wings. She spread them, feeling the air curve under them, and hopped through the shattered window to join the feast.

*Based on a plot hole in a movie I saw quite some time ago, this story*
*deals with characters whose stories were left on the cutting room*
*floor. Here's the movie I'd have made.*

## THE TRUTH ABOUT DANIEL

Daniel's wife keeps knocking at my door. I don't want to answer, I have nothing to say to her and she has nothing to say to me that I want to hear. Covering my head with my pillow, I try to tune out the persistent knocking. "Just go away," I whisper; the knocking stops for one blissful, deceptive minute. Then it resumes, harder and louder until I have no choice but to crawl out of bed and answer.

I open the door, clutching the front of my robe closed with one hand, pushing tangled hair from my eyes with the other. Daniel's wife stands there: cool, perfectly coifed and manicured, composed and serene. This surprises me. After reading the article in yesterday's paper, I'd expected her to appear, but not like this. Distress and anger are the most common emotions in situations like these. The serenity, when it rises to the surface, if ever, is almost always much, much later. I rarely get to witness its appearance.

But she seems calm, so I shrug and head to the kitchen to start the coffee machine. I feel rather than see her detached, disinterested, yet obviously disdainful glance around my tiny house. Eventually she follows me into the kitchen and sits on one of two stools at the counter, her shapely legs curling around each other, her feet in expensive Prada pumps resting easily on the chrome ring.

I ignore her, staring out the small window above the sink. The early morning sun is warm and there is no sign of the rain predicted for today; in short, another beautiful day in Los Angeles. I shrug again; it gets boring after a while. The coffee machine splutters then beeps and I reach in the cupboard for two mugs. "Cream? Sugar?"

"Black."

I nod and fill the two mugs. I should have known that she took her coffee black, even though I knew nothing personal about her. I couldn't even remember her first name.

"Darleen."

She's good, I think, setting the coffee in front of her. I perch on the other stool, sipping at mine. She curves her hands around the cup, not touching the surface, but absorbing its aura of warmth. I wait.

And she speaks again. "Things are never the way they appear."

"Is that what you've come to tell me?"

She glances over at me, her eyes reflecting the sunlight. A small garden spider crawls over the edge of the counter and stops just next to where her hand rests. She leans forward just a bit and blows on it. It doesn't move and she seems as if she's about to cry, so I scoop it up and carry it in cupped hands across the kitchen, open the door and set it on the ground outside.

"Thanks," she says quietly. "I've never liked spiders."

I nod, and refill my mug. She's not touched hers – at least not physically. "Want a warmer on that?"

"Yes, please."

I dump her now ice cold coffee into the sink and pour more into the mug, setting it in front of her again and settling back onto my stool.

"Darleen," I start, trying to sound casual, not wanting to frighten her away. "We both know you haven't come here today to waste my coffee. What do you want from me?"

She sighs. "I thought you'd know."

I have an idea, of course, of what she wants. How could I not? "Yes, but you still have to tell me."

"Ah." For the first time since entering my house, she loses some of her composure, some of her coolness. A blush seems to paint her cheek. "It's about Daniel," she says. "You need to know."

"Fine. So tell me."

It's always like this, like pulling teeth to get the Darleens of the after-worlds to talk. I don't know why it has to be this way. The whole process should be fairly easy. They show up at my door. They talk. I listen. They go away. Period. Problem solved. Sometimes these little talks even help pay the rent if the local police are interested in the information.

"Daniel has," she pauses, puts a hand up to her throat, her eyes closed, "needs." Her head rolls back slowly, sensuously; she is remembering his touch. "Maybe they aren't normal needs, but they are his and I love him. Regardless."

When her voice trails off, a vision tickles behind my eyes: her delicate white skin, reddened and bruised from his needs, his leather straps and ropes and cuffs. I shake my head and give her a warning glance. Too much information, I think. She nods, sitting straighter on the stool and the visions disappear. "Thanks," I say, taking another sip of my coffee.

"Have you ever heard of Friedrich's Ataxia?"

"No."

"I'm not surprised. It's rare, a genetic thing, a degeneration of the nerves, basically. Progressive. Starting at your toes and working its way up your body. The brain, however, is unaffected." She gives a low laugh. "By the disease, at least. But not by the horrors of watching your bodily functions disintegrate slowly, day by day." She shudders slightly and turns her head, dropping back safely into the subject of Daniel. "Eventually, I could no longer satisfy Daniel's needs."

"And so he got rid of you?"

Darleen looks shocked. "No, no, that's not it at all. He had nothing to do with it. It was I who encouraged him. At first I begged him to find someone else to take care of him, to deal with his physical needs.

"I see." I rise and pour my own cold coffee down the drain. The bitter taste lingers on my tongue. "And that someone else? Was there any concern on your part as to how that someone else might handle Daniel's needs?"

She seems shocked that I'd even raise the question. "She doesn't matter. Why should she?"

I shake my head, leaning back on the counter. "Okay, Darleen," I say, asking the question I always have to ask, "why are you here?"

"I want you to say no. When they call and ask you to consult on my case, I want you to just say no."

Dammit, there goes the rent money.

"Some things are more important than the rent." She says it as if she really believes it, as if she'd ever needed to worry about money a day in her life.

"Fine." I agree, mostly to get her out of my house as quickly as possible; I don't much like the ones powerful enough to muck about inside my head. "But while you're here, please keep out of my mind."

She nods again and stares at me with those emotionless eyes.

"Is that all?" I say, knowing somehow it isn't.

"No. I want you to help Daniel."

"No way. I said I wouldn't consult on this case, but if he did it, he's not going to get away with it, whether I help or not. You should have thought about this before, when you could have done something about it."

Her voice is small and distant. "I didn't think I'd know. I thought once it was over, it would be over."

I give a little laugh. "Yeah, death makes believers of us all."

Her delicate mouth opens wide as if gasping for air. The word I should've know better than to say hangs in the air and the outline of Daniel's wife wavers, like a heat mirage. For one brief second, I see her broken body, mangled and melding with the crumpled metal of a wheelchair, I see the car speeding away from the scene. It's a small car, cheap and beat-up, but is more than enough to do the job.

"Why would I want to help him? He's a cheater and a killer. And why would you care? You're free now, Darleen, the door is wide open, just walk away."

She sighs. "I can't. Not until I know he'll be okay."

I hate the pushy ones, the ones with a purpose, however misguided, the ones who can't let go. If you don't help them, they linger much longer than they should. And you don't get a moment's peace.

I stare at her for a long while, balanced precariously between her obvious need to believe Daniel innocent and my inner feeling that he's guilty as sin. The doorbell rings and I nod at Darleen. "Let me get this," I say, "you just stay put."

I open the door to an odd sight: a girl, in her early twenties, drenched to the bones and sniffling uncontrollably, but not leaving one drop of water in her wake. Great, I think, gesturing for her to enter, another one.

"I'm sorry," she holds out a trembling hand to me, her nails are stubby and bitten, "I didn't have anywhere else to go. I need your help."

"Yeah," I say to her as she looks around my house, "Take a number and stand in line."

She follows me into the kitchen anyway and gasps when she sees Darleen. "You? Here? Why?"

"Sheri?" Darleen knows this girl, but, given the amount of disdain in her voice, doesn't seem to like her all that much. "What happened to you?"

"He drowned me." Sheri's voice quivers.

"Who?"

"Daniel."

Darleen shakes her head. "No. Not Daniel. He couldn't do that. Wouldn't do that."

Sheri gives a little snort. "Married to him for all those years and you never knew him. Even now you still worship him, don't you?"

Darleen's perfectly manicured hand goes up to her throat again and her eyes close. She rolls her head, slowly, sensuously and exhales.

"I thought so," Sheri sounds angry now and I notice that her clothes are beginning to dry, tiny puffs of steam rising in the air around her. "Well, let me tell you about your perfect husband, babe. First, he borrows my car to run you down. Then, when I threaten to tell the police, he drowns me in my own bathtub – drugs me and holds me down under the water, that bastard. He even leaves a suicide note for me, saying that I couldn't live with the guilt of having killed you."

The certainty in Darleen's eyes begins to falter. Sheri reaches over, takes her hand. And even I, standing on the outer edge of their rapport, see the truth about Daniel. Darleen closes her eyes again, but when she opens them next, they are narrowed with anger. Hard. Unforgiving.

She smiles. That smile gives me shivers.

Still holding hands, they turn to me, their eyes gleaming with unholy anger.

"So," I say, suddenly glad I am not Daniel, "what do you want me to do?"

"Nothing." Darleen takes the lead. "I think we can handle this all by ourselves."

And without so much as a thank you, they melt away.

I shake my head. "Well, if that isn't damned annoying, I don't know what is. A total waste of a morning."

I take a hot shower to alleviate the chill of the dead and dry myself off, dressing for the day. I barely get my wet hair combed when someone knocks again.

I walk to the door, shaking my head. "What is it now, Darleen?" The knocking continues. I put my hand to the knob, "you know you could just walk right through if you wanted to…" and open the door.

"Sorry, I don't think my captain would approve."

"Oh. Detective Willard." I open the door wide, "Come on in and have some coffee. I thought you were someone else."

"Obviously." He sits down at the stool Darleen previously occupied. "Cold in here, isn't it?"

"Occupational hazard." I fix him a cup of coffee – at least this one won't go to waste. "What can I do for you?"

"It's the funniest thing," he says, "I was coming over to consult with you on a case."

"The Daniel O'Brien case?"

"You always know," he shakes his head and chuckles. "Of course you do. That's why we consult with you."

"What do you want to know?"

"Nothing now. As I pulled into your driveway, I got a call that he'd turned himself in. Confessed to the murder of his wife and his girlfriend. What a sleaze."

"Then you're just here for the coffee?"

"And the company. Like I said, I was on my way already."

I smile. It's nice to be wanted. I open my mouth to speak, and the knocking starts again. Frantic this time. Knocking like someone's life depends on it.

"Dammit."

Willard looks at me, confused. "What? Did I say something wrong?"

I throw my hands up in the air. "It's not you."

A brief frightened look crosses his face. "Oh."

"Hold on a minute." I get up, cross the room, and fling open the door.

"Please, you have to help me."

I look him over, give him an acknowledging nod. "Daniel." His perfectly tailored suit is sopping wet, twisted, and torn. Fragments of bone appear through the rips, blood mixing with the rivulets of water running down his broken body.

"Help me, please."

"Too late." A mist forms around him and hands reach out to grab him. I recognize them both: the set of beautiful nails and the grubby ones, the touch of avenging angels to drag the true Daniel to his final justice. I shiver a bit and back off. "Way too late, my friend."

Daniel screams for one brief second as the cloud envelops him, then he disappears. Forever.

Back in the kitchen, Willard gives me a questioning look. "Daniel? And too late for what?"

"Too late to help either one of us. He's gone, so you won't get the satisfaction seeing the bastard put on trial and I won't get the rent paid."

He thought for a while, then shrugged. "At least it's a beautiful day."

I take a sip of my cold coffee. "Yeah, there's always that."

*Another story written for an anthology which never came out. But now, at long last, revenge on that dreadful Count. And a vampire named Bitsy. How can you go wrong?*

## TWO'S COMPANY, FIVE'S A CROWD

I waited for my sisters in the library. It was a cold room, despite the heat of flames from the huge fireplace. In this place, all the rooms were cold. Wrapping a woolen shawl tighter around my shoulders, I held back a shiver and glanced at the maps he had left on the table. My mouth tightened and my resolve strengthened. It must be done, I told myself, and it must be done now.

Angelique arrived first, her lips drawn thin in what I'd finally realized was a perpetual sneer. She raised an eyebrow as she kissed me on one cheek and then on the other. "Making plans, Sonya?" she asked, gliding over to one of the chairs by the fire and seating herself. "Again? What makes you think they'll work this time?"

"Because they have to, Ange. We've no other choice. This situation has gone on for too long and it must stop." I looked up at the clock on the mantel and shook my head. "Where's Bitsy?"

She shrugged and tossed back hair as blonde as mine was black. "Who knows?" she said, her voice bored and dull. "Reading, perhaps. Or trying on dresses. That's all she seems to do lately. I wonder why she bothers. It's not as if there's someone here to admire her. Or any of us, for that matter."

Angelique sighed heavily -- being admired was always more important to her than to either me or Bitsy. I looked over at my sister; she deserved to be admired. Out of the three of us, she was the prettiest. And although the years had not diminished her porcelain-like beauty, I detected a loss of life in her eyes. I suspected that same loss was reflected in mine; days once filled with promise and excitement now dragged seemingly into decades. Or centuries. How dared he do this to her? Or to any of us?

I walked over to Angelique and laid my cheek on the top of her head. "Don't you see, my sweet angel? That's exactly why we've got to try."

"Try what?" Bitsy flounced into the room, slightly breathless and wearing her favorite dress. A little smile curved her full lips, the shade of which perfectly matched the red of her frock. Her hair was as black as mine and her skin as white, but while I'd been told I looked sultry and exotic, she managed to dance through her life draped in a veil of romance and innocence. "Will it be fun, Sonya?" She gave a soft laugh and looked around the room expectantly. "Are we going to play a game? Or," and her smile deepened, exposing perfectly white little teeth, "has that delightful Mr. Harker come back to call? You promised us kisses, Sonya, don't you remember?"

I nodded. "Yes, Bitsy, and you would have had those kisses, we all would have. Except..." I let my voice trail off knowing that she would finish the thought, wanting to put her in the proper frame of mind for my plan.

"Except he wouldn't let us." Bitsy frowned and flopped down onto a chair next to Angelique. "He's no fun," she whined, her voice petulant, "he never lets us have kisses."

"And it's not just the kisses," Angelique rose out of her sublime ennui to add her complaints, as I knew she would, "he won't let us leave. Ever. We're trapped in his drafty, dusty old castle with nothing to do. Oh, yes, it's fine for him to go batting around all over Europe, but we can't even go into town. It's just not fair."

I crossed the room to both of them, taking their hands in mine and looking deep into their eyes. "Tell me, sisters," I dropped my voice to a husky whisper and they both sat straighter in their chairs as I'd expected, "do you remember when you last had a good meal? One in which you felt like you'd drunk your fill?"

Bitsy groaned and patted her flat stomach through the silk of her dress. "Sonya, did you have to remind me? I'm so very hungry that the rats are starting to look tasty."

Angelique rolled her eyes; I knew she'd rather starve to death than stoop that low. Bitsy was a simple soul, though, and lived for her appetites.

"I don't think, Bitsy dear, that we need go that far. I have a plan that will ensure us plenty of kisses forever."

"Forever," she sighed. "Forever once seemed so glorious. I remember the night we met. He looked so handsome and I was young and pretty and innocent. My father thought he'd make an excellent husband. 'Set your cap for that one, Elizabeth,' father said, 'he'll do right by you.' And then we danced, he and I." Bitsy's eyes acquired a strange misty distance as she viewed her past once again, reliving old glories. "He whispered such divine things in my ear."

Angelique pushed her chair back. "Yes, Bitsy, we know. You've told us so very many times."

"But he was sweet." She looked up at me and giggled, not noticing that Ange was standing behind her, mocking her gestures and her words. "I wore this very dress that night, in fact that was the night I received my new name. He told me that I looked just like a little bitsy blood drop."

I choked back a groan and gave a warning glance to Angelique where she stood mouthing the words. I needed to cultivate Bitsy's anger and discontent, needed to channel her temper in his direction, not in ours. She was simple in her wants, true, but not stupid. And while I did not believe she would be much help in my plan, her silence was crucial. I did not want any unprotected thoughts to filter back to him. Catching the undead by surprise is not an easy trick.

"He loved me then," Bitsy continued, "I know he did."

"He never loved, Bitsy. Never." The lie flowed over my lips like honey or sweet sips of blood. My stomach growled with the thought. "The last meal he brought us proved that. Did he think that a baby in a bag would satiate the hunger of three grown women? No," I answered for her, "he didn't think, he never thinks. Then he wouldn't even let us feed on the mother when she came looking for her luckless babe. Instead he waved us away, 'Wives, go to your coffins and let the children of the night feed.'" I patted her hand in consolation but repeated the harsh falsehood. "No, Bitsy, he never loved."

I knew, in fact, that he did love. Too well, actually, and way too often, but he did love. I, also, had my fond memories of when we'd first met and the centuries of bliss we'd shared. I'd considered myself lucky to find him as he no doubt did me. We had seemed the perfect match, then, and I put up with his domineering ways, playing the properly submissive wife to his master of darkness.

All of this domestic harmony, though, had ended on the night he brought home another wife. Another wife? I still seethed inside from the memory. Did the man's ego know no bounds?

"Prepare another coffin, Sonya," he'd ordered, "I've brought us home some company."

I stared at him for some few seconds in disbelief, having at first thought he'd brought us home a late-night meal. "Company? What on earth do you mean?"

He laughed then and kissed my hand. "A sister for you, my love. I thought you'd be happy, you're always complaining that you're lonely."

"Lonely?" I thought that over. "Yes, perhaps, but that wasn't quite --"

"So then, Sonya," he said, interrupting. "this lovely child is Angelique." He paused a moment and looked down at the waif shivering in the hallway, "That is your name, is it not, girl?"

She nodded and yawned.

After that day, I'd often thought that the best thing I could have done was destroy the creature that very minute. Both of them, for that matter. But he was right, I was lonely and in time, I'd adjusted to Angelique and we managed to form an alliance against his disregard.

The addition of the third, a century later, had thrown off our balance somewhat, until Bitsy's sweet nature had won me over. I found in her, if not a kindred spirit, then at least an unformed mind that I could mold and nurture. She learned about our life under my tutelage and when she expressed an interest in the books in the library, I taught her to read. That her taste in literature ran to the romantic and the chivalrous was not my doing.

Whatever we had been prior to us bringing us together, we became sisters of a sort and confidants and soon would be conspirators. No doubt it was not the effect he'd hoped for.

But enough was enough. I caught glimpses of his thoughts, even from England. First there'd been this Lucy person, but she was easily dispatched. My sisters may have missed out on Harker's kisses, but I, of course, knew ways around the castle they'd yet to discover. Not one man, nor even one woman, ever left this place without bearing my marks on his neck and my presence in his mind.

From local gypsies to bearded Irishmen researching novels, they all proved amenable to my tampering with their wills and their viewpoints.

As a result of these shared kisses, Jonathan's sleeping mind provided me an open channel to his closest associates and from there all it took was a hint dropped to the proper person. Lucy was history and I thought the problem was solved.

I should have known better. Lately Harker's dreams had been increasingly disturbed by the attention their mysterious visitor showed his lovely Mina, newly married and in the first blush of carnal love. More horrifying was the knowledge that Mina shared the interest. Apparently, it was one thing for Jonathan to share kisses with me in a castle far away and quite another for his wife to entertain thoughts of any other man in their marriage bed. I found Harker exasperating, but we agreed on one matter. There would be no fourth wife in this castle. And if I could manage it, no second or third either.

"We need to act now," I told my sisters, "he will be returning to us soon." He was already on his way, at sea. While Harker's ridiculous friends kept up on the comings and goings of my wayward husband through the hypnotism of Mina, I managed to eavesdrop on their schemes. All I needed to do was affect one or two changes and my plot would be accomplished for me.

As their approach drew nearer, I continued to manipulate my sisters, feeding upon Angelique's boredom and on Bitsy's thirst and her hunger for romance. I painted Jonathan Harker and his friends as knights in shining armor, come to rescue us from durance vile; Mina, on the other hand, was the enemy, a vindictive woman who would be first in his attentions, his admiration. Worst of all, this fourth wife would be first in line for feeding. By the time I received the communication that the motley group had camped in a nearby forest, I had fueled their greatest fears and they were ready.

"Come, sisters," I urged them, instructing them to put on their filmiest clothing, "it's time to meet our fate."

"Ooooh," Bitsy said with a flush of excitement, "can we really go see them? Dare we leave the castle?"

Angelique shrugged, "We might as well, there's nothing going on here."

We found Mina, sitting on a log, shivering in a protective circle of communion wafers. She seemed to me rather plain and more than a little stupid, but perhaps that was merely due to the cold weather. She continually sniffled and rubbed her nose on the sleeve of her coat. For the life of me, I didn't understand what they all saw in her, but the minds of men, alive or undead, are hard to fathom.

Angelique and Bitsy amused themselves by rushing in towards her, hissing and crooking their fingers menacingly. Although we hadn't actually come to terrify the poor girl, I allowed my sisters their fun while I searched the area for our real target.

Van Helsing emerged from the forest carrying an armful of wood for the fire which he dropped at the sight of us. Fumbling in his pocket, the professor produced a large crucifix, and held us at bay as he stepped into the circle with Mina.

Angelique and I hissed a little more for dramatic effect, but Bitsy fell quiet. I noticed a slow blush crawl over her pale cheek as she stared at Van Helsing. He, in turn, gazed at her hungrily. His mouth hung open and his eyes raked over her body, taking in each and every curve artfully revealed as the wind blew the filmy material of Bitsy's gown. His face grew flushed and the light in his eyes was unmistakable.

I smiled and nodded. It hadn't mattered which one of us this man fancied, but I was secretly pleased that it was Bitsy. She, of all of us, deserved a fairy-tale rescue. Grabbing her arm, I pulled her away from the circle. "We must go now, it's almost dawn," I whispered to her, feeling her reluctance to leave. "But never fear, dear heart, he will find us again."

Van Helsing wasted little time in doing just that. I barely had time to secure our crypt for daylight and position our coffins so that Bitsy's would be the first he'd encounter, when I heard him enter the door and descend the steps. As I'd expected he came alone.

The lid of my coffin was slightly ajar, and I lay quietly watching and listening, ready to emerge at the slightest suggestion of danger. He bore a black doctor's bag and as he approached Bitsy's coffin, I heard it hit the ground, heard the sound of wooden stakes clattering to the floor and rolling away, heard the small creaking sound of a lid being opened.

"So beautiful," he whispered. "So pure, so virginal. She cannot be what she seems." Van Helsing's breathing grew heavy and he fumbled with his clothing.

Holding back a laugh, I pushed back my own lid and silently emerged, gliding over to where he stood. "Yes, Professor," I said over his shoulder, "she is lovely, isn't she?"

He jumped and pulled his coat closed, clearing his throat nervously. "Madam, you have the advantage of me. I did not know you were awake."

"Obviously. After seven centuries one does not sleep as well as one likes. But we shall not speak of that. I see that you are enamored of my sister and can assure you that she feels the same about you. Perhaps we could reach a civilized arrangement?"

I kicked the stakes and the black bag away from his feet. "Really, there's no need for violence. We mean you no harm."

Van Helsing's glance darted from Bitsy's perfectly exquisite sleeping form to my face. "An arrangement?" His voice cracked.

I nodded.

"And this lovely creature would be amenable?"

"Absolutely. Come now," and I took his arm and led him to a darker corner of the room, carefully outlining what he would need to do to dispatch the evil Count. When I felt sure he understood what I wanted, I allowed him to leave.

"Remember, Professor," I called as he ascended the stairs, "have the body delivered here tomorrow evening and Bitsy will be yours. Forever, if you like."

"Bitsy." He sighed. "Such a perfect name for a perfect creature. Rest assured, fair lady, I will not fail."

After I heard him leave the castle, I started to laugh. "Now there's a match made in heaven if ever I saw one. Wake up, Bitsy darling. Rise and shine, my sweet Angel. In less than twelve hours we'll be free."

The following evening, Professor Van Helsing, as good as his word, sent to the castle the body of my husband, complete with coffin and the gypsies, my gypsies, to deliver it, along with a letter addressed to "The Divine Miss Bitsy." Angelique happily rode away in the wagon with the two departing men, waving to me only once before turning her attention to her companions. I'd never seen her look so alive.

Bitsy emerged from the castle, suitcase in one hand, letter in the other, and bid me a tearful goodbye. "Are you sure you will be all right here by yourself, Sonya? I'll worry about you."

"No need, Bitsy. I'll be just fine." I smiled and kissed her. "Don't keep your knight waiting any longer, Princess."

When she disappeared from my sight, I turned and walked back into the front hall. The coffin stood there and I peeled back the lid to look at his face. The Bowie knife which had been driven into his heart exactly as I had instructed gleamed in the light of the torches. I hesitated, then sighed and pulled it out.

He groaned and opened his eyes. "Sonya, my love, what took you so long?" He brushed at his clothing. "I fear I am somewhat disheveled. But you, look at you. You are as beautiful as ever."

I shook my head, putting my hands on my hips. "Do not try to sweet talk me, old wolf. What were you thinking? Will you never learn? You can't go batting around with other men's wives and hope to avoid the consequences. Fortunately I was able to convince that pig-headed doctor that cold iron would kill you just as easily as wood. Or your dust would be blowing in the wind even now."

Gracefully he moved out of the coffin, took my hand and kissed it tenderly. "I am grateful. But the others? Are they here also?"

I glared at him. "Gone. And if you know what's good for you, there will be no replacements. Remember, my husband, that I made you what you are. And that I can unmake you with a thought."

Then I smiled, he was so handsome and one as old as I surely had a right to be foolish. "Besides, sweetheart, one wife is all you need. Now take me out for dinner, it's been a long, long time."

*I'd originally intended to write something called
"GhostWare," but it just refused to come together. A change of title and
monster and voila! We'd achieved story. For the record, I never read
those instruction manuals either.*

## VampWare

Sarah Barlow pushed her chair away from the computer, locked her fingers together and stretched out her arms, cracking all her knuckles in the process. She tilted her head from side to side, trying to shake out the kinks that had developed and stole a half- guilty, half-pleased look at the clock. As she'd suspected, as she'd planned, it was much too late to attend her afternoon class. What the hell, she thought, I'm flunking anyway. Why prolong the agony?

She padded down the hallway of her apartment to the kitchen and poured herself a cup of this morning's coffee, now thick and grainy. Sarah grimaced as she drank it. "And who gives a shit?" she addressed the empty room, "even with a Master's there are no jobs to be had. I'm better off here, so long as dear old Daddy keeps the checks coming in."

Sitting down at the small kitchen table she looked at the wall calendar where a countdown of red numbers marched over the current week and the next. Today was Tuesday, she was now nine days away from the deadline for her dissertation outline with nothing to show for her efforts but eight-clocked hours testing Gideon's new computer game, "VampWare."

Undaunted, Sarah picked up her portable phone and dialed his office number. As always, he answered on the first ring, as if he had nothing better to do but wait for her call.

"V.G.I, Gideon Richards speaking," he said formally. She was constantly surprised by his voice, deep and rumbling, it sounded as if it belonged to a trucker, not the delicate and pale effeminate figure that was Gideon. If she hadn't heard him speak in person, she would have bet that he'd had his office phone modified to artificially enhance his voice.

"Hi, Gid. It's me, Sarah."

"Sarah. It's early, I didn't expect to hear from you so soon. Aren't you supposed to be working on your dissertation?"

She gave a snort of amusement. "As if I could, when you keep tempting me with these computer games."

"Well," Gideon laughed, a low, strangled chortle, "candy doesn't work for little girls like you; I've had to work hard and long to find something alluring enough to keep up my quota."

"Very funny, Gid. Anyway, it worked. It's a wonderful game."

"Good, I thought you might enjoy it. How many hours have you logged in?"

"Eight, so far. And it's great, but another hour and I'll be at the last level."

"I know, it's not challenging enough for you. But I have the prototype for 'VampWare II' right here on my desk, fresh from the lab and ready to be tested by any eager guinea pig I can find."

Sarah held back a small gasp. "But you told me that wouldn't be ready for months."

"We sped it through production, just for you, my darling. And Sarah," the pitch of his voice seemed to lower even more, now possessing a throbbing, persuasive note, "this one is a virtual."

"Gideon," Sarah said, unable to control the desperate tone that colored her words, "I have to have that game."

"I know."

"So what'll it cost me this time?"

"Nothing you can't spare, Sarah. Your first-born son perhaps, or maybe we'll just settle for your immortal soul."

Sarah laughed. "Well, no problem, that you can have. Thanks, Gid. I'll be right there."

The offices of V.G.I. were just several blocks from

Sarah's downtown apartment and she made the trip in five minutes. Her normally pale cheeks were reddened from the cold, and she gave the receptionist a wide smile, combing her fingers through short, brown hair that had been tousled by the wind. "Hi," she said breathlessly, "I'm here to see Gideon."

The woman behind the desk gave her a cool, appraising stare and Sarah stood defiantly, making no effort to pull her jacket closer around her body. She was aware, but uncaring, of the inappropriateness of the skin-tight leotard and leggings she wore into the office environment.

"I will tell Mr. Richards you're here." With a final sneer the receptionist turned back to her desk and buzzed Gideon's intercom. "Ms. Barlow is here to see you again, Mr. Richards."

"Great. Send her back, Mary." His booming voice seemed to echo from the walls of the sparsely furnished lobby; Sarah gave Mary a smug smile and sauntered down the hall to his office. Half- way there, aware of the woman's still unapproving scrutiny, she slipped off her jacket and slung it over her shoulder. "If you had an ass as good as mine, you dumpy old bitch," Sarah muttered, smirking, and deliberately emphasizing the wiggle of her hips, "you'd probably walk around buck naked. So eat your heart out."

"Excuse me?" Gideon stood in his office doorway, leaning against the jamb and shook his head at her. "Talking to yourself again, Sarah? That's not a healthy sign, you know."

"Why don't you sack that old ghoul, Gid? She doesn't meet your image of a leading edge company. And what does V.G.I. stand for anyway?" Sarah went into his office and flopped into one of the black leather and chrome chairs next to his desk.

"I've told you a hundred times already," Gideon said with an exasperated sigh, "Vampire Games, Incorporated, as anyone should have been able to figure out. And you must have read it repeatedly on the game instructions."

"Oh, those," Sarah shrugged, "I never bother with reading them. I live the games."

"A dangerous attitude . . ."

"But one that you would like to foster in every home across the country, no doubt."

"No doubt." Gideon agreed and sat down behind his desk, his long, slender fingers splayed out upon the highly-polished surface. Sarah studied him for a minute; he fascinated her, he always had since the night they'd first met in the seedy student bar she frequented.

It had been a cold, misty night about a year ago and the bar had been practically deserted, most of the other students were spending one last night cramming for mid-terms. Gideon had approached her while she stood at one of the video machines. "Excuse me, miss . . ." he began, but Sarah waved him away.

"In a minute," she said, not even looking at him, "I just fed the damn thing another quarter." And he stood quietly, patiently, trying not to interrupt her concentration. But it didn't work. His presence there was so commanding and so unnerving that eventually she turned away from her game in progress, leaned up against the machine and glared at him.

The man was definitely not her type; she wasn't entirely sure if he would be anyone's type. He was tall, gaunt and his dark clothes emphasized his ashen skin. Yet, there was something oddly attractive about him, although she could not quite define what that quality was — maybe the deep-set, almost black eyes, or maybe the swatch of baby-fine black hair, that fell on his forehead, giving him a boyish appearance. His manners were impeccable and fastidious, and when he introduced himself, producing the small business card that declared him as vice-president of gaming module research and development, it seemed to her a match made in heaven.

Their relationship had never progressed beyond friendship, and that suited Sarah just fine. She had been repelled by his initial touch, that clammy hand grasping hers only briefly, and as time went on she had accepted his idiosyncrasies as part of the total package, grateful that there seemed to be no sexual strings attached to the vast wealth of material he had offered for her consumption.

Sarah's eyes darted around the office now, searching for her newest free gift. Gideon watched her intently for a moment then gave his low, rumbling laugh.

"Can't wait, can you?"

"Hell, Gideon, I ran all the way here. Where is it?"

"It's here, my impatient one." He pulled out a large carton from behind his desk. "You do understand, Sarah, that this is merely a prototype. You must be extremely careful. AND READ THE INSTRUCTIONS FIRST."

She winced a little from the loudness of his last words. "Hey, why don't you just give me the basic run-down, Gid? I'll wing it from there."

Gideon shook his head, a wry grin twisting his narrow lips. "Fine, if that's how you want to do it. But remember that you were warned."

"Warned? Against what?"

"The lab results have proven that this is an extremely addictive game. And much more complicated than the original VampWare."

"Great, I can't wait to start."

Gideon proceeded to explain the intricacies of the hook-ups: the helmet and bulky gloves that would actually bring the game to life. Sarah nodded, only half-listening, her fingers literally itching to begin. "And this is the most important facet . . . Sarah! You're not paying any attention to me, are you?"

"Hmmm?" She tore her eyes away from the high-tech equipment alluringly displayed on the desk and focused on his face. "Go ahead, Gid," she nodded, "I'm listening."

"I repeat, this is the most important facet — don't forget to set the helmet clock. Two hours is the recommended time and more than enough for your first time through, if you even last that long. The commercial version will have an automatic time-out built in, but in the prototype you must do the timing yourself. Don't forget."

"Yeah, yeah, Gid, I won't, I promise. And if I can't take the two hours, I deserve to lose."

"Well, then," he shrugged his thin shoulders, "take it and play in good health. Call me after you've clocked your first two hours and let me know what you think."

"Two hours, my ass," Sarah muttered as she cleared space in her office for the new equipment. "I'll play as long as I like." She made the appropriate connections the way Gideon had shown her, then sat down in her chair and turned on the game.

The opening screen was almost identical to VampWare I and Sarah snorted as she entered in the appropriate information when prompted. "New and improved, huh? Gideon, you gotta do better than that."

But then the words and pictures on the screen melted together to form a computer approximation of Gideon's face. The expression in his eyes was one of challenge and arrogance, and when he spoke, the inflection of his voice was scornful and realistic. "You are about to enter into the domain of bloodthirsty and terrifying vampires. Everything that you experience will feel perfectly real. The first ten minutes of the game after you don the equipment are a safe time to get accustomed to the controls and the environment. After that you are on your own."

"Thanks, Gideon," she replied as she put on the helmet and the gloves as requested. Sarah took one long deep breath and hit the enter key.

"Jesus H. Christ." Sarah's words echoed through the damp, stone hallway. "I can't believe it. It's just incredible."

As if transported miraculously, Sarah found herself in a cold and dank medieval castle, lit by burning torches and by the setting sun faintly shining through a narrow window at the end of the hall. "I see," she said, smiling, "I'm only safe until the sun sets. Nice touch, Gideon."

Sarah jumped when his voice answered. "Thank you, Sarah. I knew you'd like it. You have ten minutes, my darling, use them well."

In spite of herself, Sarah shivered. Then she noticed that she was clothed in only a white, lightweight, almost transparent nightgown. Her feet were bare and her long hair — long hair? she thought, confused — streamed down her back. "Very gothic," she spoke quieter now, so that she would not be heard, "but very unsporting. Where are my weapons? My defenses?"

"You will have to find them."

"Shit." Sarah looked at the waning sun and hurried down the hall, checking each room she passed for weapons. The first room was completely empty, as was the second. From a distance, Gideon's voice boomed, "Seven minutes and counting."

"Should have read the damn instructions." Sarah opened the door of the third room. This one contained a wrought iron candelabrum holding five candles. As she watched, one of them sputtered and burned out. "Great, less than seven minutes and it's about to get dark . . ." She left the room, and tried the next door; it was locked. She pounded on the door with her fists and a moment of panic washed over her; here she was, dressed like a 17th century bimbo, armed with nothing, about to face a hoard of hungry vampires. Then she remembered that it was just a game, a good game, one that felt real and frightening, but a game nevertheless. And she could always get out if things got too bad. It just felt like she was in this damn castle, in reality she was sitting in her apartment, playing.

"Six minutes to go, Sarah. Will you be ready?"

She laughed, "Yeah, I will be."

Finally four minutes and three doors later, she found some useful items; standard vampire protection, she scoffed, but at least it was something. A few cloves of garlic, a bottle of what she presumed was holy water and a three-foot long wooden stake, the pointed end sharp and lethal. But she had no way to carry everything and wasted one more minute trying to decide what to take. Eventually she opted for the holy water and the stake, both of which would serve as offensive weapons. The garlic she left behind.

"One minute, my sweet."

Quietly, she went back into the hallway, looking for a place to make her stand. Not by the open window, she shuddered as she watched the last rays of the sun filter through the surrounding forest, better off back where she started. That way she could get out quickly if need be. Sarah ran down the hallway, but it seemed much longer than she remembered. All of the doors, rooms and torches looked identical, the exit could be anywhere.

"Thirty seconds." Gideon's voice sounded pompous and self-assured.

"Go to hell. I'll beat this game, you'll see." Frantically, Sarah tried to remember the brief glance she'd taken at the instructions. She was supposed to flex her right hand to get the options menu, she thought. Setting down the bottle of holy water, she raised her arm, and made a fist. "I feel like a damn fool," she muttered.

"Twenty seconds, and of course you do, my dear."

Or maybe it was her left hand? She put the stake down next to the holy water, and made the same motions with that arm. Neither worked. She tried both arms simultaneously as the ten-second warning came. A gust of wind blew through the open window and all of the torches at that end of the hallway blew out. From behind her, faint but threatening she could hear the beginning of a blood-curdling hiss.

"Shit," she spun around, her foot kicking the stake. It rolled down the hallway, knocking down and breaking the bottle. Sarah felt tears sting in her eyes as she watched the wet stain that was one of her only two defenses spread out on the cold flagstones. The stake itself had disappeared into the darkness.

"Time's up."

A misty figure began to materialize next to her. When the familiar form of Gideon appeared she relaxed slightly and smiled, giving a nervous laugh. "You were right, Gid, I should have read the instructions first. Now, be a love, and tell me how I get out of here."

He said nothing, but grinned at her, exposing a set of truly realistic canines.

She backed away from him. "No, really, Gideon, tell me how to get out and I'll go back and read the stinking book. I promise."

He still did not speak, but he reached out and grasped her thinly-clad arms. The chill from his contact caused Sarah to shiver. "Gideon? What do I need to do? Tell me."

He laughed, his face closing in on hers. "You've already done it, Sarah. And now I take my payment."

"Your, your payment?"

His mouth was treacherously close to her neck, his breath was hot and putrid. "Yes," he hissed, "my payment. Your immortal soul."

Gideon's teeth came down on her neck.

And Sarah Barlow's last earthly thought was that they could have made losing the game a lot less painful.

"Graphics aren't much better than the first one." Thirteen- year old Ted Hampton said to the friend peering over his shoulder as he entered the appropriate information on the opening screen of VampWare II. Then the words and pictures melted into a picture of a woman, long brown hair curling provocatively over her thin, white nightgown. "Hey, cool!"

"You are about to enter into the domain of bloodthirsty and terrifying vampires." The woman smiled at Ted, exposing long, blood-stained canines. "I am Sarah," she said in a sultry voice, "and I will be your first challenge."

"Man, she's a real fox," Ted's friend said, "I bet you could have fun with her!" He chuckled slightly, "Maybe you better read the instruction manual before you start, Ted."

"Nah, those things are for wimps. I want to live the game."

www.ingramcontent.com/pod-product-compliance
Lightning Source LLC
Chambersburg PA
CBHW071305130626
46556CB00003B/1476